LOVE LEADS HOME

LOVE LEADS HOME

June Masters Bacher

Phoenix Press

WALKER AND COMPANY
New York

**Large Print Edition published by
arrangement with Harvest House Publishers**

Printed in the United States of America.

Library of Congress Cataloging-in-Publication Data

Bacher, June Masters.
  Love leads home.
  Sequel to: Love is a gentle stranger, Love's silent song, and Diary of a loving heart.
  1. Large type books. I. Title.
[PS3552.A257L685 1988]   813'.54   87-32854
ISBN 0-8027-2624-0 (Lg. print)

**First Large Print Edition, 1988
Walker and Company
720 Fifth Avenue
New York, NY 10019**

Send for a complete catalog of large-print publications.

Dedicated to
The Rev. Richard Huls,
my minister and my mentor.

PREFACE

Love Leads Home is the fourth (and final) in a four-novel series depicting romance and courage in the wild and beautiful Oregon frontier. Artists find it difficult to paint the region. It is so green and fertile that it lacks the contrasts of most regions. One depends on words as tools—words from such old-timers as the Irish O'Higgin (in **Love Is A Gentle Stranger, Love's Silent Song,** and **Diary of a Loving Heart**) to catch the spirit of the country.

In one of the rich valleys protected by ancient and sometimes mysterious mountains is a special settlement where **Love Leads Home** concludes this Western saga. The valley is held to its distinctly different sister-valleys by the mighty arms of the Columbia River, one of the four great streams of North America. Heading into the Canadian Rockies, the river has the strange power of becoming like the countryside through which it flows. Aimlessly it meanders through Washington, but then, as if by unseen Power, it becomes an awakened giant in Oregon—gouging through mountains with gathering force to rush to Celilo Rapids, the Grand Dalles, and into the Cascade Gorge.

Or that's the way it used to be—before its power was harnessed by the building of a dam. But the "Old River" will not be forgotten as long as folklore continues among the "Oregon children" who gather to hear repeated stories of the red men paddling up and down these white-capped rapids . . . coming of the palefaces with their wagon trains (meeting here the greatest hardships of the trip across the continent) . . . and it will not be forgotten that underneath the now-still waters of the dammed-up lake lie the fallen rocks of the natural bridge which once spanned the river, "Bridge of the Gods."

Yes, Oregon is home to its inhabitants. But in the heart of young True North, "home" could be elsewhere as well. In searching for her real identity, True feels she must go back to her mother's homeland in Atlanta . . . and then to Boston, where her father, whom she never met, was killed. But there she finds more conflicts, more displacement of her heart, and more questions. Maybe she should go home to Oregon to sort things out . . . especially three men in her life. . . .

A gentle love story, **Love Leads Home** will leave you with a more clear and inspiring definition of love . . . a loving heart which finds and cherishes all earthly love . . . . . and a more faith-filled heart which recognizes the origin of our being.

For God Himself is love!

CAST OF CHARACTERS

"True" North (Trumary North, daughter of Mary Evangeline Stein North and Wilson North's stepdaughter)

Angel Mother (Mary Evangeline Stein North, Wilson North's first wife and True's mother)

Daddy Wil (Wilson North, settlement doctor and True's stepfather)

Young Wil (Wilson North's nephew and adopted son)

Aunt Chrissy (Christen Elizabeth Kelly Craig North, second wife of Wilson True North and True's aunt)

Joseph Craig (Uncle Joe, first husband of Aunt Chrissy and settlement minister)

Marty (adopted son of Aunt Chrissy and Uncle Joe)

Grandma Mollie Malone (Mrs. Malone, wife of the Irish O'Higgin)

O'Higgin (second husband of "Miss Mollie")

Michael St. John (shareholder in transcontinental railroad and most eligible bachelor in Atlanta)

Cousin Emily Kincaid (Michael St. John's cousin and powerful ruler in the Kincaid-St. John household)

LOVE
LEADS
HOME

1

Going Home—Or Leaving It

God bless you one and all, my wonderful family. Know that I will remain with you always. I will blossom with the dogwood in the springtime and hum with my bees in the summer sun. I will sparkle with the snowflakes and in the ribbons of each rainbow. I will laugh when you laugh. Cry when you cry. So long as you are together! For I leave with you my legacy of love.

Your Vangie

• • •

The final entry in the diary of Mary Evangeline North, True's "Angel Mother."

• • •

The conductor paused to look down at the Dresden-china beauty of the sleeping girl. Must date back to royalty, this one. Only rarely did such appealing mixture of fragility and strength show up among the few women passengers, at

1

least on his run between Portland and San Francisco. The big violet eyes, so childlike, gave vulnerability to the girl's face. But the little way she had of thrusting out the rounded jaw spoke of courage.

Well, of course, this young lady had courage! Otherwise, would she be crossing the country by train alone? Why, the rails linking East and West were hardly laid before this one was traipsing to—where did her ticket say? Atlanta? That was it—Atlanta, Georgia!

The slender figure of the girl stirred as the train's whistle cut through the stillness of the afternoon, echoing and re-echoing against the autumn-painted canyon walls. As the train snaked around a sharp bend, the man heard the girl murmur something almost inaudible.

"Home," he thought she said. "I'm going home—or am I leaving it?"

A finger of sunlight found its way through the smoke-darkened windowpane, turning the pale gold braids to molten copper. The conductor sucked in his breath in admiration. About the age of his Midgie, she was. And then a frown crossed his weathered face. Sometimes he worried about his daughter. Alone there in Portland since they'd lost her mother. . . .

Suddenly aware of another presence, True North opened her eyes. Aunt Chrissy had cautioned her about strange men who sometimes tried to become too friendly. She relaxed when her eyes met those of the conductor, her self-appointed guardian. She would miss him when his run ended in San Francisco. He would go back home and she would have to change trains after a long layover and resume her journey alone to the land of her mother's childhood. True shivered with a mixture of anticipation and downright fear. Fear? Yes, she admitted it for the first time: fear . . . fear of traveling alone, and fear of what she would find when she reached the big city where she knew nobody.

Oh, it's not that she would have let Daddy and Aunt Chrissy know. Or, for that matter, Marty (had she known his whereabouts), or the twins. And certainly not Young Wil! He had opposed her leaving like this more than all the family.

"True, you are out of your mind!" he had said, his brown eyes showing more emotion than usual. "At your age—"

"Leave my age out of it!" True had snapped. "I'm 19!"

He raised a submissive hand. "All right then, a girl—"

"That, too!"

I wouldn't have been so snappy, True thought now, *if I hadn't been about to cry. . . .*

True came back to the present with a start. Conductor Callison was speaking.

"Anybody meetin' you when you change trains?"

"No, but I'll be all right." She had said the

same words over and over to her family so much that they were automatic.

The conductor took off his cap. His large head with the silver mane of hair wagged back and forth. "I don't know about young folks these days. Worries me havin' you girls out on your own. You and Midgie need men looking after you, what with danger lurkin' around every corner."

True turned back to the window. She'd heard all about his daughter. She did not want to hear it again. Already she would recognize Midge Callison if she met her aboard this train . . . gray-green eyes, slanting upward at the corners "like her mother's, rest her soul," lots of heavy, dark hair "done up fancy-like," but not easy to understand—his Midgie . . . but there was a young man now . . . and he was hoping . . .

True kept nodding politely, concentrating all the while on wiping away enough film on the window to make a peephole through which she could catch one last glimpse of the beautiful Columbia River below. She succeeded just as the train's whistle gave a last shrill warning and turned sharply to begin its long, tortuous crawl up the mountainside. Her beloved river lay like a silvered mirror below. Bordered on both sides by mountains, the trees seemed to float on the surface as the late-afternoon sun turned their needled boughs from green to gold. A lump rose to her throat. She couldn't be homesick already.

To get herself under control, True turned her attention back to the fatherly man beside her.

"I'm going to miss you," she said. It was true. No matter what pretense she made at being independent, inside she was scared out of her wits.

"It's been a pleasure, miss—a real pleasure," he said with a pleased smile. "I still think young ladies as pretty as you hadn't ought to be runnin' around alone, but—" Mr. Callison paused, scratched his head as if in despair, and put his conductor's cap back on.

Then, seeming to brighten, he said, "There's somebody aboard I'm hopin' to introduce if ever his business is finished—shareholder on the railroad and—er, well, most attractive."

"Most attractive" would mean *male, unattached*. Well, *no, thanks!* The last person True wanted to meet was a man, attractive or otherwise. And she had her reasons. She had given up trying to make Mr. Callison understand that she had had enough experience with young men. True found herself confused sometimes trying to figure out the relationships. Marty, adopted at birth by Aunt Chrissy and Uncle Joe, must be a "cousin." Yes, that was right, *cousin;* because, even after Uncle Joe's fatal accident Aunt Chrissy had married Daddy Wil following Angel Mother's death, that would still be right—wouldn't it? And, as for Young Wil—oh, dear! He was Daddy Wil's nephew, so what *did* that make him to her? *Cousin? Stepbrother?* She only knew that they

5

were *family*, and that she loved them very much—except when Marty was a brat and Wil was so bossy. . . .

"I—I—" True began. But the conductor was gone. Just as well. It was all so confusing. She turned back to the view below, watching every detail—half-wishing the train were going the other direction. Closing her eyes, she saw the family. . . .

Lost in thought, True was unaware that the conductor had returned until he spoke. "Like I said," he began, "you ought not be alone in all them big cities. Should have a man at your side as a—well, means of protection—"

"I don't need protecting." If she kept her eyes closed, maybe he would go away.

Mr. Callison cleared his throat and tried again. "There's someone you oughta be meetin'—"

"I don't *want* to meet 'a someone'!"

"How can you know when you haven't even met him—I ask you, now, *how?*"

The man had been a gem. Getting started on the long journey had been the hardest part, and he had taken her under his wing. But now he was doing what Mrs. Malone back in the settlement would have called "over-eggin' the pudding," and it was adding to her misgivings, just as Aunt Chrissy, Daddy Wil, Marty, and Young Wil had done. It was best that she set things straight once and for all. She was intelligent, self-sufficient, and *determined*.

6

"Really, Mr. Callison, I am capable of being very rude. If you come dragging some man up here, I am apt to prove it!"

"You just did."

Startled by the strange, male voice—low, throaty, and deeply amused—True bolted upright, her violet eyes wide with surprise and embarrassment. To add to her confusion, she felt hot color stain her cheeks. Before her stood a tall, sandy-haired stranger, hat in hand, and hazel eyes twinkling with amusement.

Bowing low, the young man said, "I am that someone!"

2

No Longer Strangers

The conductor introduced Michael St. John as a shareholder in the railroad line between Portland and San Francisco, and then hurried away on his duties. True wondered if Aunt Chrissy would consider it a proper introduction. Perhaps she should dismiss this man with a glance or a word—no, she had been rude. Good breeding demanded an apology first. So thinking, she turned to the man who seemed to be waiting for her to make the first move.

She met his eyes, then blushing, glanced down. His gaze was bold and complimentary—out of keeping with the boyish-looking face.

True inhaled deeply in preparation for trying again—and quickly, lest this man get the impression that she was engaging in the age-old game of letting eyes meet as if by chance, with each glance exchanged becoming a little longer. She had never engaged in flirting. But she had watched other girls, and she knew the pitfalls.

When she lifted her eyes again, there was no mistaking the pleasure in the beginning of a smile below his closely cropped mustache. There was an uncomfortable knotting of her stomach mus-

8

cles—the kind that came whenever she met a new man.

One would think the year in Portland would have given her more poise. Fumbling for her bag, True pretended to look for a lost item. When Michael St. John laughed softly, she realized that he had taken her behavior for affected, mischievous disdain—a mistake that must be corrected, and quickly!

"I owe you an apology, Mr. St. John," she said with gathering courage. "I'm afraid I sounded abrupt. You must think me a terrible prude."

"Not at all," he said, "but may I sit down for a moment?"

True hesitated.

"I assure you that I don't eat young ladies. Poor digestion, you know."

Surely there could be no harm in that.

"Of course," she said, trying to sound hospitable but distant.

"Now," he said, easing into the seat beside her and crossing one gray-checked leg over the other, "I have a theory about the little wrongs we commit. It's not enough to apologize. We need to go back to Point A and proceed cautiously until we find where we went wrong, then correct it."

"I don't understand."

"Well, I should have asked the conductor to get your permission before disturbing you. You, on the other hand, feel that you were rude—so

9

I suggest that we start all over. I want us to be friends. How do you do, Miss North?"

True laughed. It undoubtedly was happening too fast, but he *was* entertaining—

Without awaiting a reply, Michael St. John continued, "I am Michael to my friends—and may I call you True? Someday I would be interested in knowing how you came by that name."

Again, True felt color creep into her face. Her name was something she would never discuss with anybody, excepting Young Wil.

They had read the story over and over in her mother's diary . . . talked about their pasts together . . . and gathered the rest from Daddy Wil and Aunt Chrissy. But it concerned nobody else! Without realizing it, her chin went up in defense.

The look was not lost on the young man beside her. "I've a feeling the lady guards a secret," he said as if the idea pleased him. "But, alas! She will never confide in me until we are no longer strangers. Should I tell her now that I am 25, the most eligible bachelor in Atlanta—"

"Atlanta! Atlanta, *Georgia?*" True's heart picked up a speed that was frightening.

The man who wished to be called "Michael" smiled. "Is there another? Not to us natives."

Unaware that her blue eyes were like twin violets in her excitement, True whispered breathlessly, "Natives—you're a native? Because that's where I'm going!" True blurted out, regretting

10

the impulsive words immediately. How forward the man would think her. "I—I mean, it's a coincidence," she finished lamely.

"My good fortune," he assured her. And, to her relief, he had failed to notice anything amiss in her words, it seemed. "I seldom get out this direction—second trip, in fact. But my father's health is failing and he has shifted most of the railroad business to my shoulders. Most of my traveling takes me to one of the branch offices since the consolidation. So I divide my time between home and Boston."

"*Boston?*" The word was a whisper.

"You've been there too, I gather. I had no idea you were so widely traveled—but, again, my good fortune."

"I've never been to either city," True said slowly, wondering how much to tell him. "My ancestral roots are there."

"Then I take it you'll be staying with relatives?"

Relatives? True was not sure she had any. In her bag she had all sorts of names, maps, and family history, but she still was not sure where she would be staying in Atlanta. Perhaps in a suitable boarding house. . . .

True realized then that Michael St. John was looking at her quizzically. Then his expression turned to one of friendly concern.

"Never mind, I foresee no real problem. Atlanta has built back considerably since the war

11

between the states. Many of the old mansions are still intact, and the owners take in boarders. By the way, would you care to join me in a late supper? I have a partial coach, such as it is, near the back and—"

"Oh, no—no, thank you," True said quickly. "I have enough food with me to furnish a diner."

"Which we'll have once we change trains in San Francisco. The rails out West are newer, you know, and as yet lack the modern conveniences. I shall insist on your company once we are aboard for Atlanta."

"That would be nice," True said, feeling a thrill of excitement. It was hard to believe her good fortune—meeting someone who could help her change trains and find a place to stay in Atlanta.

Could he also help her trace her ancestry in both cities? Of course, she would have to work carefully, revealing only so much.

There were things one did not discuss outside her family.

"I shall say good night, then—and I'm glad I met you, True North. The gods were smiling on me this day!"

"*God*," True corrected softly before offering him her hand. "I'm glad too," she added—"glad we're no longer strangers."

12

3

To "Point B"—And Beyond

The mirror in the section marked "Women's Powder Room" was cracked, and some of the silvering on the back had sluffed off.

Even so, True's reflection was reassuring. Aunt Chrissy would have discouraged her from changing clothes so quickly. The long leg of the journey lay ahead, and she would need several changes. Well, she wasn't responsible to her mother's sister or anybody else now. It was essential that she make decisions on her own if she were to accomplish her mission this first time away from home.

Well, not the first, exactly. There had been Portland while she prepared herself to follow in her aunt's footsteps and become a teacher.

But alone? Never! Not with Young Wil to lean on, confide in, and lend a broad shoulder when she cried herself dry of tears when she was homesick. She was going to miss Daddy Wil's nephew—*so* much.

True squared her shoulders determinedly. *Stop it,* she told herself. *Stop it right now! He saw you as a little girl!* She had thought he saw her as a young woman until he realized she was really serious about making this trip into her past.

That hurt. It hurt maybe more than saying good-bye to the rest of the family. His opinion had always been her mirror. . . .

She must take one last look at her reflection and get back to the coach. Michael St. John had spoken of bringing coffee from his compartment, and it seemed only proper that a lady should look her best.

Yes, the front view was fine—dark skirt unwrinkled and flaring out at the bottom as it should. Blouse—well, becoming. She was right in changing from the navy polka dot to the white, tucked-in-front one with the deep yoke and elbow-length sleeves. It was "the acme of elegant simplicity," according to the mail order book from which she had ordered.

Somehow she thought Michael would like simple things. Oh, it wasn't that she was dressing for *him*, True assured herself, as she took a small compact from her bag and, turning her back to the mirror on the wall, examined the back of her hair.

It was good that the women in her family had no need to resort to the puffs, wigs, and switches shown in Portland. But she did wish her hair would stay in place and stop curling like a schoolgirl's around the nape of her neck and tumbling down over her forehead in front. It made her look younger than she was. No wonder Young

Wil felt so superior—as if eleven years older made him so.

Then, contradictorily, she thought, *Oh, Wil, I miss you so much!* She owed him so much—always knowing her thoughts, her wishes . . . only *he* would have known how much it meant when he located the family brooch and bargained with the Portland jeweler for it. He had cautioned her to have the valuable pearl-and-sapphire piece of jewelry locked in the train's safety box for her own protection in case of train robbery.

Train robbery indeed! she had scoffed, feeling that such talk was only another scare tactic to keep her from making the trip.

Gone was the need for bravado. In its place was a longing to hold onto something tangible—something that tied her with her family back in the Oregon Country.

Pulling the brooch from her bag, True looked at it with the usual fascination. Always she had loved it, even before knowing its full history. The blue lights of the sapphire seemed to light the dismal room. And then, on impulse, she pinned the heirloom on the bosom of her white blouse before stepping from the powder room to wait for the young man who had been so kind to her.

Back in her seat, True took the small Bible she always carried from her bag. As usual, she read the fading message from Aunt Chrissy to

Uncle Joe, given to her then-new husband when he accepted his first ministerial position.

And, as usual, her eyes misted over. Brought up in a loving environment of family and friends, True had always been "best friends" (as she, Young Wil, and Marty called themselves) with God. But it was dear Uncle Joe who had baptized her in the shallows of the valley's river. He held a special place in her heart, as did each member of the unusual family to which she belonged.

How did one hang a label on love, anyway? There were so many kinds, and she loved each of the wonderful ones in the Craig-North family differently.

Almost, but not quite, she could identify the special feeling she had for Young Wil. But it was best not to try.

Pushing the idea into a corner of her mind, True opened the Bible. Almost automatically it opened at the Old Testament page from which Uncle Joe had read at the close of her baptismal: "The Lord bless thee, and keep thee: The Lord make his face to shine upon thee, and be gracious unto thee: The Lord lift up his countenance upon thee, and give thee peace" (Numbers 6:24-26).

True remembered wishing Marty had accepted the Lord along with her. He had refused, and she had felt very lonely in spite of the crowd on the riverbanks—lonely, that is, until Uncle Joe took her hand in his big one reassuringly and read the Holy Words. Almost symbolically, a

16

mourning dove had flown over the water that orchard-scented spring day. And she was no longer alone.

"Good morning, True North!" The voice was rich with feeling, but low, as if the young man she had met yesterday had no wish to startle her again. "May I offer you a cup of morning coffee?"

True smiled a good morning and accepted the tin cup gratefully.

"You have been most kind," she murmured, dropping her eyes when she saw the look of admiration in his face. His own eyes traveled from the pointed toes of her button shoes to her upswept hair. Then slowly they came back to rest on the bosom of her blouse. She felt herself color under the scrutiny.

"My pleasure—and you will forgive me for staring, but that is the most beautiful brooch I have yet to see. The sapphires must have been chosen to match your eyes."

True hesitated, taking a small sip of hot coffee before answering.

"I'm afraid the jewelry was purchased long before my time," she said. "My mother's—a gift from my father—"

"I'm sorry if I've embarrassed you. Those blue eyes illuminate a certain sensitivity I want to explore after we progress to Point B!"

We have—and on beyond, True thought, un-
certain whether to be happy or frightened.
He reached across and closed her Bible.

4

Growing Fear

It was hard to determine how much time passed. There seemed to be a lot to talk about, considering that Michael St. John was a stranger.

Of course, people who traveled together had an opportunity to become better acquainted than those who met casually on occasion. At least, True told herself that was why she confided more in him than she had intended to.

The man was easy to know. Or was he? Something gave True the feeling that, although his eyes crinkled often with a smile and his manner suggested good-natured candor, he held something back, especially when he talked business, which he tended to do after polite encouragement.

But invariably the conversation came back to True. It was flattering but embarrassing—and more than a little disconcerting. There was a lot which True planned to keep to herself—and for good reason.

Did her father or her mother live in Atlanta—or was it Boston? Both places, True explained guardedly. Was either still there? No—her father was dead . . . and there she stopped.

Even after all these years, it was hard for her to say that her mother was dead. So she had kept the childhood image created during her years of formative theology.

"You mentioned an uncle and an aunt in Oregon. I gather you have been staying with them while attending school in Portland? Tell me, did you like teaching?"

"I only taught a part of one year—Aunt Chrissy's unexpired contract," True answered quickly, hoping that he would not push further into why she was in Oregon, or why she chose to go to Atlanta and Boston.

Let him think she was "visiting" Oregon—or whatever he might be thinking. Better that than saying she was going back to trace her way, if possible, to her mother's and aunt's home (where they both had been hurt so cruelly) and to search for her natural father's grave—the man who was responsible for their broken hearts.

"Tell me about your work?" True said, putting more enthusiasm into her voice than she felt in hope of steering the conversation away from herself. She met Michael's eyes.

Tall and broad-shouldered, with well-groomed hair framing his face, he had looked stern in repose. Now the handsome face lighted up as if in response to the flare of excitement in his hazel eyes.

Obviously, here was a man who loved his work. And obviously he had done well in the railroad business. His clothes had a tailor-made look and he wore them with the confident air of a man accustomed to wealth.

True tried to concentrate on what he was saying.

"As you know, good times did not climb the Rockies and smile on Oregon. When the gold boom failed, settlers—so my father tells me—began blaming their troubles on the railroads. There was plenty of beef, lumber, fish, apples, and even mined goods going to waste without the railroads, which were bringing prosperity to other regions. Well," Michael said as he combed his blonde hair with his fingers, "am I boring you?"

"Oh, no, not at all!" True said truthfully.

Laying a light hand on hers momentarily, as if in gratitude, he allowed it to remain only a proper time and then resumed talking.

"When cross-continent rails were first planned, things looked rosy. We're traveling on a spur of the first efforts—but quarrels broke out and there were those like Ben Holladay who controlled the stages between Missouri and the Oregon frontier—ever hear of him?"

Hear of Ben Holladay? True smiled, remembering the wonderful winter evenings when Daddy Wil and his Vangie (before she became "Angel Mother"), Uncle Joe, and Chrissy used to gather around the fire and dream of the prosperous days ahead as she, Young Wil, and Marty monitored the conversations. The railroads would come through. Produce would be hauled away. The mill the men co-owned would flourish. The Pony Express would come on to Turn-Around Inn to delight the O'Higgin Malone clan . . . steamboats . . . the land flowing with milk and honey, they'd said. There would be a growing need for Daddy Wil's medical services as a doctor, and certainly there was always a need for God-called ministers like Uncle Joe . . . on and on went their cotton-candy dreams, their low-pitched but excited young voices echoing softly against the time-mellowed beams of the great living room of the North home, where True was born. The children's eyes would droop sleepily . . . but her mother had captured the dreams in her diary.

True came out of her reverie with a start. Michael St. John had stopped talking. Guiltily she looked at him. What had he asked? Oh, yes, Ben Holladay.

"Forgive me," she said, "but the name brought back memories. Please go on. It won't happen again."

Was the look in his eyes annoyance? Amusement? No, it was something else. More curiosity.

But why? Then, to her relief, Michael was speaking again.

"Well, if you're sure?" When she nodded, Michael went on: "Holladay bought up a line of steamships running between Portland and San

Francisco, then decided to build railroads. Big spender that he was, he built a mansion, brought in Eastern people, and filled the lobbies at the State house—only to go bankrupt.

"Along came Villard, sharing the grand vision with Holladay that the Pacific Northwest would become a great empire. All it needed was railroads. They had the mistaken idea that if the country would fill up with people, the rails would pay off."

Michael laughed, as if the idea were amusing.

"But wasn't that part true in a sense?"

It seemed important somehow that she know if the laugh had been directed at the immigrants. Did he think that money determined *worth?*

He shrugged.

"People with money, yes. But some of the people were pretty low-lifed—"

Anger rose inside True—a defensive kind of anger that refused to be denied a voice. Her words, when she spoke, however, were low and calm.

"I fail to see the connection."

Michael, apparently unaware of her strong feelings, simply shrugged again and went on with his railroad history. Northern Pacific crews building across Montana at the rate of three miles a day . . . killing off buffalo . . . and at last driving the "Golden Spike" which linked East to West . . . then his family had bought shares

23

from them all and "come in for the kill" . . . but there were still hard feelings. . . .

"Oh, I doubt it," True said. "The Oregon people are too grateful to hold grudges about squandering of some of the pools to which they contributed—and, besides, they aren't like that. They are friendly and warmhearted—"

"Not when it comes to having the railroads run through their lands, they aren't!" Michael's eyes lit up strangely.

True sucked in her breath. "If you mean the few train robberies—"

She paused and held his gaze.

"I do!" he said. And something in his tone frightened her.

Change of Plans

"San Fran-*cis*-co!"

When Conductor Callison sang out the words the next morning, True eagerly raised the faded blind to see the waking city.

Her first glimpse was one of disappointment. Smoke emitted from the slowing train mingled with the early-morning fog to enshroud the city.

Then, as the train came to a hissing stop, the smoke cleared and she was able to see enough to make her gasp with wonder.

Almost surrounded by water, enthroned on hills, San Francisco seemed to go on forever. She had read so much of the city's landlocked harbor, one of the largest in the world, according to her geography teaching manual.

Oh, it would be so wonderful if she could see it even from a distance! Her students would want to hear all about it. *If* she went back, True reminded herself. At any rate, she would want to tell Young Wil about it in that long, long letter she had promised him.

Strain as she would, however, True was unable to see the water of the bay or the ships it hosted. The dense fog persisted, seeming to billow in like clouds and settle around the tall buildings, climb the steep streets, and become a a part of the sullen skies.

Depressed by the scene, she was about to turn away in hope of seeing Michael St. John when the conductor came into the coach again. He paused at her side.

"Unable to see Alcatraz on a morning such as this, I s'pose? Easy to confuse 'The Rock' with a battleship—lonely island, isn't she just?"

Shivering, True nodded. Recently printed history books had a lot to say about the disciplinary measures taken in the barracks.

"Military prison, isn't it?"

"Yep—oh, there she is, a little to the north!"

With mixed feellings, True turned her face to the direction Conductor Callison pointed. In the distance she could make out the faint outline of what indeed did appear to be a ship. Then the fog closed in. Something about the scene tore at her heart. It looked so cold. So lonely. And, unaccountably, she felt the same way.

It was the weather. It had to be the weather. "Grandma Mollie" Malone would be complaining of her rheumatism and Daddy Wil would be assuring her she would feel better once the sun broke through.

But they weren't here. And she was alone—unless Michael showed up, as he had promised. True longed to ask his whereabouts.

The conductor would know. But that might seem forward—

And then she saw him!

At first True thought it was only her imagination. This fog was tricky, winding itself like evil fingers around anything it seemed to touch. But then, as if enjoying the game, the fog moved on, only to thicken again.

It had parted long enough, however, for her to see distinctly that it was Michael St. John.

Michael and three or four other men, all well-dressed, wearing hats and carrying canes and briefcases, standing together as if in an important conference just outside the coach behind her. And then the others had moved away like the fog, leaving Michael standing alone.

Mr. Callison had seen, too.

"Makin' arrangements for changin' trains and the like, no doubt," the man said, seeming to feel a need to explain. "I just learned from the switchin' yard that there'll be no layover for you. Real blessing—probably time enough for coffee. Me, I'm glad I was able to find a fine-appearin' young gentleman to look after you on that long, lonely trip. If 'twas my Midgie—oh, here's Mr. St. John!"

True made a futile effort to sweep the tendrils of curling hair from her forehead, a motion not wasted on Michael.

"Leave it alone—please do," he said with a warm smile. "It's very becoming, you know.

And I'm happy to see you're wearing that splendid brooch again."

I'm wearing all the clothes I wore yesterday, True thought with embarrassment. There was so little time. And certainly the ladies' room afforded little space or privacy for a lady's toilette.

True thanked him and then asked anxiously about the change of trains.

There was no cause for concern, he assured her. He would see to it personally that she was safely aboard and comfortable. Oh, very comfortable! His eyes narrowed slightly as if he were about to reveal a secret.

He had strange eyes, she found herself thinking. Sometimes they were amused. Often they were pensive. And today as he talked with the strangers there in the fog she had observed a certain shrewdness she had not seen before. She knew very little about this man really. . . .

Which was the same way he felt about her, True realized with a start. For his next words caught her completely off guard.

"Just who are you anyway, my Mystery Lady? You know, it occurs to me that you have told me very little—about yourself, I mean."

True studied her hands. The nails needed buffing. "There's nothing to tell," she said, buffing a thumbnail across the folds of her long, dark skirt. The skirt had picked up lint, she noticed. She must look a fright. . . .

True paused. Then, realizing that he was wait-

28

ing for more, she made a hasty decision. It would be better to handle the problem lightly. He was not one to be put off.

But she couldn't help wondering what his reaction would be if she told him the real story of her life. Not that she intended to. Now or ever!

"Really, Mr. St. John," True said coyly—glancing up to be sure Michael knew it was a game—"my name, as you know, is True North, age 19, of good family and excellent health. None of my family has been hanged—"

His laugh sounded forced. "There's more to your life story—"

True interrupted with a light chuckle.

"Yes, oh yes! Lean closer and I will share with you that I am a—*shh-h-h*—teacher! I am earthbound and I am a free spirit. That's about it."

Michael was no longer smiling.

"Banter is fine, up to a point. What I had in mind was this. Are you betrothed?"

A strange warmth crept through True's body. She might have known where the conversation was leading. Here she was avoiding one issue and another cropped up.

When she did not answer, Michael leaned forward to look into her face.

"Is there someone *else*, True?"

Use of the word "else" startled True. That meant *he* was interested.

Why, they had just met. There could be no doubt that the relationship was moving too fast.

It was dangerous in more ways than one, particularly since they would be running into one another either by arrangement or design.

A shrill warning whistle sounded, jolting True back to the present. If she should miss this train—

Involuntarily, she reached for her bags and would have risen to her feet except Michael St. John sprang up ahead of her, blocking her passage. The suddenness of his movement and a certain glint in his eye was startling and a little frightening.

"Really—I must go," True said quickly. "Please let me pass."

Michael did not budge.

"I shall in due time. But not until I have my answer."

"You have no right to ask—"

Another blast of the whistle rose above the sound of foghorns.

"That's not quite true," he said. "You see, I am about to offer you the use of my headquarters from San Francisco. And certainly I have no desire to be getting myself into one of those triangles where somebody gets shot!"

"I have no idea what you're talking about. But I do know we must go—*please!* But, no, there's nobody else—at least, nobody to whom I am engaged to be married—not now anyway—"

Michael's hazel eyes were suddenly dark.

"There *is* a rival, but I take it not a serious one at the moment. Very well, then. Now to explain. I've been detained and you will use my coach."

6

Beginning of a Fairy Tale

Leaning back against the fringed cushions of the velveteen couch, True tried to put into proper perspective everything that had happened since her tearful good-bye to her family until this moment.

It was impossible, of course. How could she put events in order when she was unable to recall events themselves?

Michael St. John's handsome, slightly mocking face floated around the luxurious compartment of the private coach—smiled at her from the gold-framed mirrors, glowered from the silver-gray of the shirred, sateen drapes, and studied her every move from the soft glow of the shaded gas lamps.

What on earth was she, True North, fresh from a homespun community in the Oregon Country, doing here?

A mellow toot of the southbound train assured her that she was not dreaming. Perhaps it would have been better that she had been. There had to be a price to pay later. Things like this just did not happen in real life. And then in panic she tried to recall where her host had said they would meet.

"Get hold of yourself, True North!" she said aloud sternly. "You wanted to be on your own. Well, you are. You very much are!"

With that, she felt inside her handbag to make sure Michael's note bearing his aunt's address was there. She relaxed when her hand closed around it. Of course, it would be in the small compartment right beside her Bible.

Feeling better, she took out the Bible and decided to read until supper was served, as the porter had told her it would be. But she did not open the Bible right away. Something else troubled her about Michael St. John.

Why had he deliberately closed her Bible on one occasion? The incident had gone unnoticed at the time, but she remembered it now. True found herself wondering if he were a Christian. Somehow she doubted it.

Well, that was sad. Just as it was sad when *anyone* had missed the joy of knowing the Lord. Michael belonged on her prayer list. But she was going to explain to God just why he was on that list—and it wouldn't be because of any personal interest in the man!

Still . . . she was grateful to him. But for Michael St. John she would be in one of those straight-up, green chairs in an overcrowded day coach (probably half a dozen cars away from the ladies room and maybe leading through the men's smoker!).

So she must thank the Lord for bringing this stranger to her. At peace with the thought, True began to read.

A light rap on the door interrupted her reading. The knock was followed immediately by the tinkle of a chime.

"Last call to dinnah, Miss No'th, ma'am," a soft-voweled voice said outside the door of the compartment. "Mistah St. John s'posed you'd be wantin' dinnah in his qua'tahs? 'Stead of the dinah?"

True closed her Bible and hurried to the door. There she was greeted by the white-coated porter who had introduced himself as "Mose" during the rush of her getting settled in the elaborate coach and Michael's hasty departure from the train.

Unaccustomed to such service, now True could only stare at the beautifully laid-out tea cart with the starched lace topcloth not quite covering the pewter bud vase holding a single red rose.

When she nodded mutely, Mose's ebony face wreathed with smiles which showed rows of startling white teeth. Immediately he rolled the tea cart in, uncovered it, and began to lift lids from the silver tureens.

"Here, I'll do that!" True said quickly.

Mose shook his head doubtfully.

"Mistah St. John he won't be likin' that. The mastah dun said—"

True smiled.

"I appreciate your loyalty to your employer, Mose. But he is not your master! Only the Lord is entitled to be called by that name."

The black man smiled shyly. True wondered as she took the silver serving spoon he was holding if he had never received a compliment before.

"Yessum," he said and smiled again.

Before leaving, Mose opened a lavishly curtained corner which converted into a little booth—a private dining room—surrounded by brass rails which held the curtains.

True was glad she was to be alone. She was sure the food would be unfamiliar—sure, too, that she should have dressed for dinner. The closest thing she had which qualified as a dinner gown was the tea-rose taffeta that Aunt Chrissy and Grandma Mollie had hand-stitched for her. Aunt Chrissy had mentioned several ladies' shops in Atlanta which used to offer a seamstress for a reasonable fee but cautioned that the fire during the war had most likely taken them.

Well, her clothes would have to do. Nobody else was going to know her identity anyway.

Correction! Michael St. John knew too much already . . . oh, how had she gotten herself into this web?

Aware suddenly that Mose was waiting to be dismissed, True murmured a thank you. When the door closed behind him, True turned to the table.

No matter how it had happened, she was here. And it *was* a glorious adventure—maybe just what she needed as prelude to the search for her real identity—not the identity she knew intellectually, but the one she must know in her heart before she could decide where she belonged.

She wished again that Young Wil had been more in favor of this trip. But he, having no desire to locate his wayward mother who had deserted him when he was a baby, was unable to understand her quest. Her letters would win him over . . . beginning with the fairy-tale existence on the train.

But as to how it came about? What would he think of her accepting favors from a strange man? Well, *fiddle-dee-dee!* He saw her as a sister. He saw her as a child. He saw her as a sometimes-pest. So why not shock him into seeing her as a grown-up young woman capable of managing her life?

Aware that she stood foolishly in the center of the little booth with the spoon in her hand, True seated herself, hesitated a moment, then lowered her head in silent prayer before lighting the candle beside the rose.

Then she took in the sight that danced before her in the candle's glow. Salad of shredded carrots, slivered almonds, baby corn, and miniature shrimp . . . chicken soup laced with some kind

36

of creole seasoning . . . and whatever could this main dish be? Certainly it was a display of color . . . bright yellow cheese sauce over still warm muffins, surrounded by turkey rolls with broccoli filling. Alongside this medley was an enormous lettuce leaf accented by what appeared to be fresh pineapple and strawberries! Another tureen held crepes stuffed with mushrooms and seafood in some kind of sauce.

True caught her breath in a mixture of admiration and despair. How could half the world as she knew it live like this while the others lived in need? Which were the lucky ones?

It's a shame, she thought, *that my fairy tale has to be spoiled!* True wished she were less sensitive to the inconsistencies of the two worlds. Food, but not for the hungry. Except her!

As if in a dream, she picked up her fork.

7

Unexpected Delay

In a very real sense, True wished the dream could go on forever—that the glass bubble in which she was encased could float high, high above the world and all its inevitable problems. For the luxurious quarters afforded her were indeed a bright bubble.

But bubbles burst suddenly, or else they fade and die. They never, she was sure, reach a point beyond the pull of the earth where they are free to orbit forever in happy weightlessness.

Like a bright bubble, True gravitated between gravity and levity. One moment she was light-headed and giddy. But the next, like a bouncing bubble, she was brought back to stark reality. Her surroundings were temporary at best. And before her lay all the problems she had brought along plus newly-created ones.

For one thing, there was the matter of meeting Miss Emily Kincaid. At Michael's urging, she had taken the elderly woman's name and address. Now there were misgivings.

What would this aunt think of a total stranger's descending upon her without warning? Maybe

Michael would send a telegram, she thought hopefully. That would prepare Miss Emily.

But True herself would be unprepared. Back in the settlement one took gifts when calling. Aunt Chrissy had failed to tell her what the customs were in Atlanta. Of course, they would have changed considerably since Aunt Chrissy and Angel Mother were there as young girls. They would have left when they were about her own age.

What would life have been like, she wondered, had they remained in their Southern home, one of them marrying Jonathan Blake? She wondered which one it would have been of the two young women—Christen Elizabeth Kelly, whose engineer-father had perished in an explosion, or her own mother, Mary Evangeline Stein, the second-marriage daughter?

Even now True's heart would not accept her mother's father as a grandfather. A grandfather gathered his offspring close and loved them. He did not reject his daughter just because she was misused by a man she trusted and, in her innocence, loved.

How could Jonathan have done such a thing? Been engaged to Aunt Chrissy, only to betray both her and Angel Mother . . . and how did she, proclaimed the brightest member of her class in both Centerville School and Portland Normal School, entertain ridiculous ideas that maybe the man still lived . . . even that one day he—rich, famous, and remarkably handsome—would come riding up in a stylish carriage to bear her away, the heir of her rightful fortune? Especially when she didn't want to leave!

Anyway, men didn't claim illegitimate daughters. Still . . .

In her younger years, True recalled as she watched the green hills give way to a flattened, sun-baked valley. Young Wil had been patient. He had called her "highly imaginative" and had told her she should write a book, as he was doing in botany. Then, after the quarrels began when she emerged into young womanhood, he had cautioned her to rid herself of the foolish "adolescent fantasies." She had become infuriated and, at one point, bitten him in the hand.

Marty had thought her wild imaginings were exciting. And he had loved the way she tore at Young Wil with words and teeth! But it wasn't Marty's approval she wanted . . . it was Young Wil's. . . .

Aware suddenly that the train had slowed, True forced her mind to slow with it. Undoubtedly, they were about to start upgrade again. Or the locomotive could be taking on water at one of the watering tanks. They were far apart.

So thinking, she leaned back and took out her writing tablet. All resentments toward Young Wil were gone. She wanted to begin her letter—one that would give the facts and more. No matter what decisions she was to reach, she needed his help—and something more, which she was unable to identify.

My dearest Wil:

True looked at the greeting. She had never called her stepfather's nephew anything but "Young Wil." But that would sound rather foolish in a letter, wouldn't it?

Maybe it was time he used some of his own medicine—outgrew her childish name for him. So let the shortened version stand.

You would never believe all that has happened! You thought I would be alone and in danger, and that is not the case. First, the conductor took me under his wing and then I met a young man. . . .

True reread the last line, frowned, and crossed out *young*. She was in the midst of telling him in detail what had happened and describing the elegant coach she was privileged to occupy, when there was a loud knock at the door followed by the sound of men's voices.

None of them belonged to Mose. Who could be wanting her?

Quickly she closed the tablet and laying down her pen staff, True was about to cork the ink bottle when the knock was repeated—louder, more insistent. And something in its sound caused her heart to beat a little faster.

Prepared to steady herself against the motion

of the moving train, she was aware suddenly that the train had stopped. Something *was* wrong!

"Yes?" she managed to answer without opening the door.

A deep-throated voice on the other side said, "Open up, lady!"

For a moment she hesitated. Just what did a lady who was traveling alone do under such circumstances? Well, Aunt Chrissy and later Angel Mother had made it alone by stagecoach. She could make it by train!

Lifting her chin bravely, "Who is it?" True asked.

This time another voice spoke. The accent was softer and the tone more gentle.

"No need for alarm, miss. We are officers of the law."

True opened the door a crack. The uniforms, all different, were reassuring. But she had not expected to see so many men in the group. Not certain what was expected of her, True nodded a greeting and waited.

"Do you want we should inspect your quarters, ma'am—er, miss—er—" one of the younger men stammered.

"Whatever for?"

"Just a routine inspection at this point," another of the officers said. "Miss—"

"North," she supplied. "Is this customary?"

"In these parts, yes—but unless you have seen something which aroused your suspicions—"

"Suspicious characters, he means. *Train robbers.*" The younger man spoke again. His voice was overly dramatic.

True relaxed a bit. The whole idea was ridiculous—so silly she wanted to laugh. Train robbers indeed! Just how was she expected to recognize one?

But the desire to laugh dissipated with one of the older men's next words. Spoken quietly, they carried a heart-chilling warning.

"This is Jesse James country."

Jesse James! but she thought the Missouri-born outlaw belonged farther in the Midwestern states.

"Are you all right, lady? Look mighty pale. We didn't have a notion of scarin' you, just cautioning you—and, by the way, 'twould be best if you put that piece of jewelry you're wearin' in safe keepin'."

Automatically, True's hand went to the brooch pinned to the lapel of her dark jacket.

"I'm all right—I guess," she said, aware that the trembling of her hands gave her away. "It's only that I thought Jesse James and his brother were captured—and certainly I never expected them here—"

"Them outlaws ain't gonna be took alive," the gruff-voiced man with a heavy growth of beard said. "And they can be anywhere. Governor Crittendon's got a reward fer 10,000 dollars dead or alive. They've joined up with the Younger Brothers now and could be anywhere. Yep, anywhere, so be careful, lady! Travelin' alone ain't recommended. Ain't safe anywhere."

It was sometime after the men left before True was able to bring herself under control. She brushed her hair and took a sponge bath. That should have relaxed her, but she was unable to eat much of the carefully prepared food Mose brought later.

And her dreams that night were troubled.

8

Trouble Ahead!

Busy with her letter to Young Wil and fascinated by the intricate patchwork of changing scenery, True lost track of time. As the conductor kept telling passengers that they had entered another Standard Railroad time zone, she would set her watch forward—thinking all the while that she had entered a time zone all her own. The past no longer seemed to count. Neither did the future or what it held.

She all but forgot her mission, except in her subconscious mind, because of the new world of elegance that surrounded her. Repeatedly she felt an overwhelming desire to pinch herself awake, only to wonder if she really wanted to wake up after all.

I'm no snob, she kept telling herself, *but is it wrong to enjoy this?*

For awhile there were feelings of guilt. Then the feelings gave way to pleasure—temporary, she knew—but maybe that's the way all pleasure was.

So, living in her personal "time zone" of the here-and-now, True was surprised when the conductor announced that they would be arriving in

Atlanta the next day. The terrain had changed to deep woods, most of the trees garbed in the sad-sweet red-golds of autumn.

But where were the swamps that Aunt Chrissy had spoken of? The bayous, switch cane, and mosses? Some trees had been cut away for the railroads, others destroyed during the war. Maybe the rest wasn't like her aunt remembered it either. . . .

True wondered sadly if Oregon would change for her in the same manner. Oh, it mustn't! It was the most wonderfully beautiful country in the world, populated by the world's most wonderful people!

A wave of homesickness swept over her, and she was about to give way to tears when there was a sudden jolt of the compartment in which she rode—a jolt so sudden and severe that it set the overhead gas lights in frightening motion and all but threw True to her knees. A prickle of fear ran down her spine.

Grasping the side of the chair where she had been gazing pensively out the window, True tried to pull herself up. But there was another jolt—a shuddering which she could hear running through the entire train. And then stillness which said the train had stopped.

Steam poured from beneath the train, making it impossible to see what was going on. True could only guess the worst.

Jesse James and his gang! They were about to be robbed.

Her first reaction was to tear the brooch from the lapel of her jacket—pricking her finger painfully. Oh, why hadn't she listened and had the piece of jewelry put into the safe?

Quickly she stuffed it into her handbag. Then, realizing that her finger was bleeding, she stuck it in her mouth just as there was an insistent knock on the door.

True's first reaction was to ignore it. If she didn't answer, maybe the robbers would go away. It wouldn't work, she knew immediately.

So, paralyzed with fear, she forgot to remove her finger from her mouth, and asked incoherently, "Who's there?"

"Conductor, miss! Sorry about the delay. Just wanted to let you know there's trouble with the tracks. Crews ought to be here soon. Suggest you stretch your legs a bit. Could take a bit of waiting when there's trouble ahead."

Weak with relief, she leaned back against the cushions until her heart resumed its normal pace. Even then, her legs were still wobbly when she tried to stand.

Maybe Young Wil was right. It was best for a man to be along when a woman was traveling.

What nonsense! she was telling herself the next moment. There had been no danger at all. Just silly fear—fear he had helped bring on by all those silly warnings!

Determinedly, she smoothed her hair in place and brushed the wrinkles from her skirt as best she could. A walk through the other coaches would do her good. Maybe she could find another woman and make small talk while they waited.

It struck her then that she had no idea how many coaches the locomotive engine pulled or what the accommodations were like.

There were countless cars, True was soon to realize, but very few passenger coaches. And crossing between the coaches was frightening. She felt that she was walking without support when forced to cross alone. But crossing when others were present was even more frightening.

Bewhiskered men seemed to enjoy inhabiting the small enclosures—all of them staring openly, a few grinning suggestively. Panicky, True hurried past them each time, dreading the time when she must retrace her steps to the safety provided by Michael St. John.

She was growing to appreciate him more and more.

The two coaches she passed through on her way toward the back of the train were a disappointment. How few women there were! And none of them gave signs of wishing to be bothered with company. They were surrounded by large families of children whom they were attempting to pacify with unpalatable-looking, stale food. Most of the men looked up with interest, but she avoided their eyes and moved on quickly.

Head down, True almost bumped into the conductor, who approached from the rear of the train. She murmured an apology and was about to move on when his hand, placed lightly on her shoulder momentarily, detained her.

"I wouldn't be going any further, miss," the man advised, pointing a warning finger at the lettering above the entranceway.

True's blue eyes followed his finger and then widened, turning violet in their surprise. The sign read: BLACKS.

"Does that mean—" she began.

The portly, ruddy-faced conductor nodded.

"Niggers. Sorry. Tried our best forbiddin' 'em, but it was sure to come even before the government mandate. Rest assured they won't be botherin' you in the dining room or powder room."

There had been actual apology in the man's voice—an apology which was misdirected. Trying to hide the annoyance she felt, True spoke in low tones.

"But how do you expect them to manage—I mean—" she stopped, embarrassed.

The conductor snickered.

"They're herded together in th' rear car. How they *manage*, as you so delicately put it, is their problem!"

Hot words rose to her lips. But it was not the conductor's fault, she supposed. His job was to carry out orders.

But if the colored people were still in social bondage, then the Civil War made even less sense than she and Young Wil had thought when they read of the killings and burnings.

Marty, on the other hand, had found all the war stories more fascinating than Aunt Chrissy's Bible stories and fairy tales. But Marty was always a strange one. While Young Wil pored over the Latin terms in Daddy Wil's medical books or labeled a new leaf in his botany collection, Marty drew pictures of cannons and interrupted her studying with his explosive, "Boom! Boom! Boom! Surrender or you'll all be blasted to bits!" She wondered where he was and what he was doing.

"Something botherin' you about the niggers bein' on the train with you, you so fine a lady 'n all?" It was the conductor's voice.

Something was bothering her all right. Her mind had wandered. But all the while a part of her had refused to allow her to turn and start back to Michael St. John's private compartment.

"Would you mind if I went in there?"

The eyes of the conductor narrowed and the furrow in his brow deepened.

"Yes'm, I would mind. I would mind very much. I promised Mr. St. John I'd be lookin' after your needs—"

That came as a surprise. Doggedly she continued, however, as if directed by some force greater than herself.

"I appreciate that, but I see no reason why I wouldn't be safe among them. I hardly think they would be that hostile."

The light hand on her shoulder tightened, slowly but surely turning her around.

"Not *them* I'm speakin' of. But the others. White folks in these parts don't like their kind associatin' with niggers—"

"Please don't use that name!"

The words were out before True knew she was going to speak.

The conductor looked surprised.

"You'll be pardonin' me, ma'am—er, miss. I never realied you felt different. 'Course, you're not from these parts."

True felt herself being firmly propelled back down the aisle as he continued.

"Main reason, though, is that 'llowing you to go in back there would cost me my job. Too near pension time for the risk."

True stopped and turned to face him.

"You mean—"

"I mean Mr. St. John would have me fired for not lookin' after you proper. Come on, now. Let me escort you back."

True did not know why she reacted as she did. Perhaps it was the nagging thought that she had let herself become too indebted to Michael St. John already.

"That man has no right to take over people's lives the way he does!" she said hotly. "Yours.

Mine. Everybody's, the way I see it! For your sake, I will obey your wishes. But let me assure you that Michael St. John will hear from me loud and clear when we meet again!"

Then, when she saw the look of pleading in the man's eyes she added an additional statement.

"Not about you, sir. I will only let him know he has no hold on me!"

Anger gave way to exhaustion. The walk back seemed an eternity. Once back inside the private quarters, True felt unutterably weary and depressed.

9

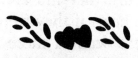

Robbery!

The day dragged on. True read her Bible, choosing passages suggested by her aunt's first husband, "Brother Joseph," whom the settlers had loved so much. Uncle Joe had penciled notes in the front of his Bible, and she had copied the references before leaving home.

When in sorrow, read John 14 . . . *Men fail you*, Psalm 27. . . ."

Quickly, letting her finger slide down the list, she located the ones she wanted.

When you want courage for your task, read Joshua 1 . . . *When the world seems bigger than God*, read Psalm 90 (and finally) *When leaving home for labor or travel*, Psalm 23 and 121.

True read the passages. Then, closing the Book, she prayed for each member of her family, admitting to God that no remnants of her mother's family in Atlanta or her father's in Boston could ever replace the people who had loved her, nourished her body and soul, and taught her of His unconditional love and forgiveness. She prayed for courage in what she herself was undertaking. She thanked Him for bringing Michael St. John into her life and asked God to touch Michael's heart if they were yet strangers.

Somehow there seemed more she should say about that, but she was unable to put the thoughts together. About to close her prayer, True remembered her rude awakening earlier to what she saw as injustice and possible suffering among the black people in this part of the world.

"Forgive them, Father, for they know not what they do," she said of the white people responsible. "If there is something I can do, just whisper it in my ear, Lord."

Feeling better after her *Amen*, True continued her letter to Young Wil. As she wrote, the hunger grew so strong to see her childhood idol that she wandered far from the facts of her journey and dipped into her storehouse of feelings—the way the two of them had always done.

As she wrote, True was aware of the *pick-pick-picking* outside her window. She had been too engrossed in her meditations and the letter to Young Wil to notice more.

But, pausing now, she was aware of singing. Beautiful singing! The kind she remembered hearing in the settlement when the black families came through.

"Goin' over Jordan and what did I see? Comin' for t'carry me home. . . ."

Rising from the couch, she walked to the window. In the gathering twilight she saw a large crew of smoke-streaked faces, beads of perspiration rolling from their foreheads. All black.

Why? True wondered. *Why?* Something was going on here—something she did not like.

Why, the situation now seemed more unhealthy than what Aunt Chrissy had described during the time of slavery! She and Angel Mother had grown up with a mammy whom they dearly loved and respected.

She would find out more from Michael . . . he had shown *her* great compassion . . . but what about others?

It was growing dark. Was that why everything was suddenly so quiet? Mose had not come in to light her lamps. And, for that matter, supper was late. She was more than ready for the train to get underway.

But why was she feeling so apprehensive? Maybe another turn through the coaches—no, wait!

Did she or did she not hear a woman scream? Probably her imagination. But the thought decided her against another stroll.

And then without warning the door burst open. Unable to grasp the reality of three masked men standing before her, their faces caked with dirt mingled with sweat above the red bandannas and hair matted to their foreheads from days in the saddle, True could only think dully that she had forgotten to lock her door.

Her next thought was that someone was playing a joke, trying to keep passengers amused until the journey could resume.

But when she saw the three guns aimed directly at her, she realized that this was the robbery of which the officers had warned!

"Keep your head, lady, and you won't git hurt," the tallest of the group said, his beady eyes boring into hers.

"This is a holdup," he added unnecessarily.

"Don't stand there gapin', lady!" The older man with shifty eyes stepped from behind the first speaker and raised the barrel of his gun. "Want that purty face blasted off?"

The taller man stepped forward again, pushing the other man's gun barrel down.

"Easy, pardner. Our pals'll take care of the rest of the crew like they done that nigger boy in th' prissy white suit—"

"Mose! You've hurt Mose?" White-faced, True faced him.

"Seems he was kinder sweet on you—and no wonder, boys. Take a gander at this one! Never mind about the black boy, girlie—git your cash out, lady. *Now!*"

Paralyzed with fear, more for Mose than for herself, True was unable to move. But she must! Her life depended on it.

For a wild moment, her mind sought an avenue of escape. Train windows too small. Crew injured—maybe some dead. She was alone. And she must find a will to move. To cooperate.

"I don't have money, just a small amount—"

The two men laughed coarsely as they started toward her. The third man slunk in the shadows.

"Ain't no mistake and if you value that purty neck, you'd best be forkin' over the dough before one of these guns goes off! Think we don't know it's the rich shareholders that ride in this grand style? I'd sooner shoot you than a sidewinder, and don't be forgettin' it—you've took our land, busted our fences, ruined the range—"

"There's been a mistake. I can explain—"

The taller man sprang forward, his movement so quick that True was thrown against the couch as he grabbed her hair and yanked her head back furiously. Pain shot through her neck and for a moment the room whirled in black confusion.

"Git your bag if I decide to let go—hear?"

Biting her lip until she felt the salty taste of blood, True tied to nod her head.

"Please," she tried to whisper, "just let me go—and I'll do what I can—"

" 'Course you will. You see, boys? Git a move on, kid!"

At the command, True was aware that the man who had stood in the shadows moved forward uncertainly.

The man holding her hair commanded, "Empty that bag of hers there on the table."

He bent his face frighteningly near to True's, pressing his unshaven cheek against hers and pulling her body close.

57

"You know, it might be wise if we just took you along fer security—and fer other reasons—understand?"

She understood only too well. And understanding caused her blood to curdle.

"Please," she whispered again. "Please, you're hurting me—"

Maybe the yell of triumph from the younger man who had stayed behind until ordered to dump the contents of her bag saved her life. True was never able to remember clearly what happened next.

The shifty-eyed man moved over beside the younger man, grabbed her pearl-and-sapphire brooch, and yelled, "Whoopee! Will you take a look at what she was hidin'!"

"Aha!" The younger man's eyes lit up with new interest. "This is no ordinary woman we have here." His tone was mocking. " 'Tis a lady, she is! Either a shareholder in this railroad or," his eyes roved about the compartment, "his mistress! What say we take 'er along—good way of teachin' 'im a lesson and collectin' us a ransom at the same time!"

There was a round of laughter while True stood rooted to the spot. Fear of what the men might do to her and heartbreak over loss of the precious piece of jewelry and all it stood for had taken its toll.

But something else had moved in to dull her senses to fear and loss—the fact that the eyes, seen only in the shadows, of the youngest of the gang were familiar. The man was someone she knew.

It was terribly important that she get a good look—*terribly* important, some flash of insight told her. She must make every effort. . . .

But at that moment there was a shrill two-fingered whistle from the mouth of a rider outside the window. So there were more, True thought dully—not that they mattered. She had to get a better look at the young man.

Maybe she would have except that her captor let go of her hair so unexpectedly that she felt her neck snap. An overwhelmingly dizziness resulted, and before she could regain her equilibrium the three men were gone as suddenly as they had arrived.

Reaching out to steady herself against the table where her empty handbag lay, True stooped to look out the window.

There, to her surprise, was a large party of men—all masked—riding sweat-soaked horses. The horses were stamping impatiently, causing dust to swirl and eddy up around their bellies, and the men's masks made them look much alike.

Except for the man standing in the center! Even at a distance, True could see that he looked out of place in their midst, dressed immaculately and wearing a rakish beaver dress hat.

If only she could see better! Straining her eyes, True tried to see his face. And then one of the horses bolted. Someone fired three shots, probably a signal, and the gang was gone.

In the whirlwind of dust they left behind, the well-dressed man was lost. When the dust settled a bit the man was gone.

Who was he? What part did he play in this?

But, more importantly, whose eyes had she seen above the bandanna when the three men broke into her quarters?

Then she dismissed her fears and brought her pounding heart under control. She had escaped with her life. What more could she ask? And with that thought True realized that others might not have fared as well. Mose, for one, was hurt!

She must get into the coaches and help. But there was a need for strength—lots of it.

"You'll have to help me, Lord," she whispered. Then, with as much courage and dignity as she could muster, True North left her compartment and walked calmly down the aisle.

"My mother was a nurse. My stepfather is a doctor. Let me pass," she said, using a gentle but authoritative voice.

The soft command had an immediate effect. White-faced mothers who had been moaning in shock and terror seemed to borrow of True's strength and busied themselves comforting their crying children.

Nobody was injured in the first coach, and, after asking the occupants to sit down quietly unless they were willing to help, she moved to the next one.

There a group of men was busy untying the hands and feet and removing the gags from the mouths of the engineer, conductor, and brakemen. Once freed, they too moved forward to check on the other passengers.

"Here's the first-aid kit, miss," the conductor said, handing True a box. "Ain't a doctor on board, but I got a doctor's kit of sorts—some ease medicine and ointments in the caboose. Can you manage 'til I go for 'em?"

True nodded, then looked around her. The woman on her left had a bad bruise on her forehead. Cold pack. Was the child's arm broken? Better splint it as best she could. She worked rapidly, all the while wondering about Mose.

And then she saw him! Lying between two rows of seats, he was so limp and still that at first she feared he was dead. Quickly, praying all the while, she felt for his pulse. Finding it, she bent to check his injuries. There was a jagged cut on his face, but the wound seemed to be superficial. Blood was seeping through his jacket, however.

With her handkerchief, she stopped the flow of blood, then ran to meet the conductor for help.

10

Strange Appraisal

Although exhausted, True was unable to do more than doze after the terrible nightmare had ended and a degree of normality had been established throughout the southbound train.

She had been awake since the first gray blades of morning knifed through the window blinds. Listening to the noisy *clackety-clack* of steel against steel, she reviewed the incidents of the night before.

None of them made sense. There had been warnings and danger signals, but none of them prepared her for the awfulness of the desperadoes who had robbed and wounded so many of the passengers. The victims, her tired mind realized, were those who appeared to be the most affluent.

But it could have been worse. *So* much worse! The outlaws could have taken her with them . . . could have killed their victims so there would be no witnesses. Who was the well-dressed man? *And whose eyes had she seen?*

Pulling herself up on her elbows, True lifted the blind and looked around her at the smoky beauty of the mountains the train had entered during the night. The first rosy fingers of sunrise touched the peaks to mingle with the blue haze.

This must be the Blue Ridge portion of the Appalachian chain she had heard Aunt Chrissy talk about so much! But, even as she watched, the chain terminated abruptly to appear again and again in short purple ranges and detached peaks.

"Does one have to pray with her eyes closed, Lord?" she whispered. "This scene is too beautiful for me to miss. How great You are, Lord—how great! Great enough, I know, to put some of this beauty into the lives of those who view Your handiwork!"

The train had picked up speed in the sharp descent of the Blue Ridge. True saw that it was now crossing what appeared to be a swamp. Moss-covered cypress trees and gnarled tupelo gums huddled together, seeming to shudder with fright at the giant Iron Horse which invaded their land.

And then a crude sign loomed up, the misshapen lettering reading: SUWANEE RIVER.

Oh, yes, the river that Angel Mother and her natural father had crossed to seek privacy. . . .

But this was no time to work at trying to put together the puzzle that was her life. There was the more recent past to deal with. And then the strange meeting that lay ahead with Michael's aunt.

Hurriedly, she pulled a robe around her shoulders and began the 100-stroke brushing of her hair.

"Miss North!" True, recognizing the conductor's voice, laid down the hairbrush and answered his knock.

"I come to invite you to the diner, miss. Hopin' you don't mind under the circumstances."

True knotted the cord of her robe and, sweeping her hair back, opened the door a crack.

"Of course, I don't mind!" she said quickly. "But the others—how are they?"

"A miracle," the man said, shaking his head with wonder. "In all my born days I never had a prayer answered so quick! I prayed for an angel and there you was—a fine lady like you, makin' the rounds like—"

"Oh, come now, please don't go putting a halo on my head. I did what any caring person would have done—and your words, well, they embarrass me, sir."

Then, lest he feel scolded, True asked quickly how Mose was progressing.,

"Oh, good as new, that boy! Them folks got a tough skin, you know—"

Not wishing to hear any more about "them folks," True said politely that she would join him shortly. Then, padding barefoot back to the dressing table, she picked up her hairbrush . . . 88, 89 . . .

True jabbed the hatpin into her flat-topped felt, smoothed her rumpled skirt, and picked up her suitcases. Foolishly, she had hoped that Michael would find a way somehow to be here before her arrival.

The morning haze had risen from the river to create a strange fog that mingled with the smoke of hissing trains. Hundreds of them, it seemed! She was surrounded by the black monsters.

It was a strange contrast to the little depot where Daddy Wil had flagged the midnight train and, surrounded by a loving family, she had boarded—how long ago?

It seemed like a million years. . . .

"Can I hep you-all, ma'am? You-all want I should call a carriage?" a rich voice asked at True's elbow. Gratefully, she handed her bags to the capable hands of the elderly, dusky-skinned man.

Feeling increasingly alone, True watched for some familiar landmark from her mother's diary or Aunt Chrissy's descriptions of Atlanta. There were none.

In place of the mansions they mentioned there were charred ruins in the midst of weed-grown lots, rotting fences with sagging gates, and neglected magnolia trees which looked as if they had forgotten how to bloom.

"This part's a heap bettah," the driver said

suddenly. With that promise he pulled the reins to guide the horses into an area which either had escaped the worst of the Atlanta fire or had been built back. Gardens were groomed to perfection. Fall flowers crowded one another for space. And giant oaks appeared to link their arms in leafy bowers above the widely separated mansions which centered the immense estates.

The carriage stopped with a jerk.

"Miss Emily lives heah," the driver half-whispered, as if afraid he would awaken the occupant.

True stiffened with surprise and half-fear.

Here? Why, this was a mansion . . . a great, white-pillared mansion . . . and she was here to meet a woman whose name she had never heard just days ago.

The hand she gave the driver was shaking and cold, and her legs wobbled as the two of them walked toward the massive white door after he helped her from the carriage. Her sense of adventure gave way to uneasiness.

Michael had made it sound so simple. True had found herself a little excited as she tried to imagine his maiden cousin. At least she would have one friend.

But now she was no longer sure it was a good idea. There was something forbidding about the place, unwelcoming in spite of its Old-South grace.

The intrigue was gone and she was on the verge of telling the driver she would return with him.

But the door opened before she could decide about ringing the chimes. It was as if eyes were watching from behind the heavy gold drapes.

A black butler in full dress opened the door but was pushed aside immediately by a circle of other people.

"I'll take over, Hosea," a softly musical voice said with a note of dismissal.

The owner approached, and even as True appraised the other woman, a part of her was unaware of pierccing, measuring eyes surrounding her.

She must be standing in the center of Michael's family. A group of "instant friends"? An anchor to cling to in case her plans crumbled?

Somehow she doubted it. If only she could escape . . . well, she would, at the earliest possible moment. Right now she must introduce herself and explain if she could.

But before there was an opportunity, Miss Kincaid was speaking.

"I am Michael's Cousin Emily," she explained. "And I bid you welcome to this house—"

"But—but—" True began uncertainly. "You don't know who I am—"

Cousin Emily's laughter was mellow, reminding True of evening chimes.

"Oh, but I feel I do! Michael's night letter was glowing with excitement. But, come, come, let us not be standing here at the door. You must meet the others here."

Then, turning, Miss Kincaid directed her words to the driver, her tone becoming clipped and abrupt.

"What are *you* waiting for?"

The driver! True had forgotten him completely under the seemingly hostile observation of her hosts. Remembering that she had neglected to pay the man, she suddenly realized she had no money. The robbers had taken all except that pinned to her corset.

"I-I'm sorry," she whispered, feeling a hot flush creeping from her neck to her cheeks. "You see, there was a problem—and my money was taken—at least," her flush deepened, "any that I can get to now—"

"So the lady needs a loan?" One of the men stepped forward, obviously a relative of Michael's because they resembled each other greatly. He bowed to her almost mockingly and his tone said more than he asked.

Is that ALL you want of us?

He paid the driver. True thanked him. And Emily Kincaid motioned the group to the parlor. As they gathered in the vast room, True was aware only of the modernization which had gone into its renovation.

It was a blend of the old and the new, with the kind of workmanship which required more than skilled workmen. Only an architect could do it—and architects charged handsomely.

But that was no deterrent to this family, apparently. And "this family" meant Michael's family, she thought dazedly. *Michael!* What had he told them, anyway?

Later, during the course of the odd conversation, True was to think a bit more coherently, taking in every detail of her surroundings—the intricate carved mouldings above the great marble fireplaces (*three* of them in one room) and the Tiffany windows alongside; the high-arch ceiling; the soft plum-and-apricot hangings; the fine paintings in heavy gold frames. . . .

But for now it took all her strength to concentrate on the people around her and try to make some sense of her strange position.

"You come as a complete surprise to us, you know, my dear," Emily Kincaid repeated.

"I'm sure," True murmured, not sure what was expected. Words were poor tools in such a situation. All she was able to manage was to stare at Michael's cousin.

The slender woman stood as tall as True. Her skin was like finely webbed parchment but was kept magnolia-white, undoubtedly by expensive creams and use of parasols to ward off the sun. The regal head was crowned with heavy hair, not braided and wound about her head like Aunt Chrissy's, but pouffed on the sides and piled on top in curls.

Cousin Emily's dress was lavender silk with a creamy white bertha laced with black velvet ribbon. Beside her, True felt dowdy. Out of date.

And untidy in her travel-wrinkled suit. Her hair needed a rainwater shampoo. Her nails needed buffing. And she felt that her usually pink-and-white skin must be streaked with soot. Else why would they all be looking at her so intently?

"Now, tell us about your trip, my dear . . . oh, forgive me, I must introduce the rest of the family. Sit here beside me."

Emily sounded cordial and at the same time commanding.

Numbly, True sat down at the opposite end of the velvet couch. Cousin Emily made an arc around the room with a slender, jeweled hand. True would never remember the names—cousins, she supposed. No closer, since the woman made a point of Michael's being an "only heir." Later she would meet his father, who was confined to his chambers . . . but for now, she must need a cup of tea, poor child. . . .

Cousin Emily rang for the butler and ordered tea and crumpets. Hosea was back almost instantly, setting out the sparkling silver tea service. Once tea was poured, Cousin Emily leaned back against the pillows and repeated her request.

"Your trip. We want to hear all about it—and you."

True fumbled nervously with her teacup. She disliked tea without sugar, but her hands were trembling too badly to risk spooning sugar into her cup.

"There's little to tell," she began. Little that would be of interest to this group, she felt. But a look around the room told her that they were interested spectators. Vaguely, she wondered why.

The silence became embarrassing. Obviously, they expected her to continue. So, choosing her words carefully, she told of the interesting scenery. Maybe small talk would suffice.

But no. The man—hadn't Cousin Emily called him Oscar?—who had paid the driver leaned forward.

"You spoke of misfortune. Did someone take your wallet?"

There seemed to be nothing left to do but tell of the robbery. It was not an interesting account, True felt. She was troubled by the focus of so many appraising eyes. She avoided telling her reaction to Mose's injury, her assistance to the injured, the well-dressed man she had seen with the outlaws—and certainly her feeling that she had seen a pair of familiar eyes.

Later, True realized that she had also avoided mention of when she and Michael had met. She had no idea what he may have told the family.

But she had a fair idea of the wrong conclusions they would draw if they knew that she had been so brazen as to occupy his quarters on such short acquaintance.

There were questions, mostly for conversation, except for the excited ones posed by two small children who had entered.

Then, without warning, an auburn-haired woman about her own age said, "North? The name is unfamiliar. Was your father from Atlanta?"

"No, my mother," True said quickly, then added, "and my father was from Boston. That is one reason why I am here—to sort of trace my ancestry. The Kelly and Stein family—"

"*Kelly—Stein—*" Cousin Emily's voice was little more than a whisper, and her face had grown pale. But she recovered quickly.

"We must ask no more questions. You must be exhausted. I shall have the maid draw your bath, because, of course, you are to stay here! You're one of us now."

One of them? Something was wrong . . . something she must correct. But for now she was exhausted. Wrong?

Of course! They were looking at her as would a groom's family. And there wasn't a groom!

11

Mistaken Identity

Tisha, one of the several maids, brought a breakfast tray the next morning. True was scarcely aware of what she ate. She was too overwhelmed by the cherry-wood furniture against the silk-covered apricot of the walls, the beige carpet with apricot-and-plum roses, and the vases of silk flowers.

Soft pink-gold sunlight filtered through the curtains drawn against the sun, giving a soft lampglow to the guest room in which she had slept.

But she did not belong in this mansion. Today she must leave. . . .

Her thoughts were interrupted by a knock. Michael? Could it be Michael? It occurred to her that the man was a stranger. With a thudding heart, True reached for her robe.

But it was Emily Kincaid's voice.

"May I come in, True?"

The tone of voice presupposed an affirmative answer. The older woman entered before True could respond.

"And did you sleep well, my dear?"

Emily, elegant in a morning dress of muted

blue, moved about the bedroom, opening drapes of the windows which looked out onto a wide veranda lined with swinging baskets of blossoming vines that formed a green screen to create an underwater look.

The antique furniture was arranged formally, and behind it True could catch a glimpse of well-manicured hedges, all ignoring fall and in brilliant bloom. A huge fountain centered the scene. It was all so lovely that True could only gasp with sheer pleasure.

"It's lovely," she murmured.

Emily Kincaid only nodded. Then she seated herself on the slipper chair near the bed.

"And now," she said, "I should like to hear about your family."

For a moment True felt a little flare of anger. What did her family have to do with this? Why was she under inspection here?

But immediately she put the thoughts from her mind. After all, she was a guest in the house. She had accepted their hospitality. And, yes, she remembered suddenly, she had mentioned tracing her past—even mentioning the name of Kelly, Aunt Chrissy's father, and Stein, Angel Mother's father.

Now she regretted that. She could never bring the cruel man who was her grandfather into her heart. Never in a million years! Why, he had hated Aunt Chrissy, his stepdaughter, and had thrown her own mother out when he found her "with child" out of wedlock. . . .

What would this woman say if she knew I was that child . . . what was it people here used to call illegitimate children—"briar-patch children"? Except that I'm not illegitimate. Angel Mother married Daddy Wil so I would be a True North! True's chin went up defensively.

True was suddenly aware that the other woman was studying her closely through narrowed lids. She colored under the level gaze that seemed to penetrate the invisible wall she had built around herself.

"Your family?" Emily Kincaid prompted.

"Yes—my mind was wandering, I'm afraid. I'm sorry—"

Why was she apologizing and what for?

"There is little I can tell you. What I mean is that I am here to sort of—well, retrace their past." She hesitated, and when her hostess did not speak, True added without necessity, "Which would be *my* past."

"I can help you," Emily said without expression. "You see, I knew your—er—Mr. Kelly, whatever relationship he was to you. He and I kept company once upon a time—which is of no consequence. But it is not my past we are tracing."

She paused, and True wondered in the moment's silence if *investigating* would not have been more appropriate. But there was no time to concentrate on the interest these people showed, for Emily was speaking again.

"It would help if you had brought along some photographs."

Maybe the woman would help, after all. It was worth a try and, besides, there seemed no graceful way to refuse.

"I have one or two," she said, fumbling in her handbag. Seeing her wallet, she paused. "I have money now, and I want to repay the man who came to my rescue yesterday—"

Emily waved a slender hand—her way of dismissing an idea.

"Your Cousin Oscar would not dream of accepting it."

Your Cousin Oscar! What on earth . . . with all her heart True wished she knew more of the practices here. Maybe everybody was "Cousin"—after proper examination.

Then, locating the pictures, she turned her attention to what had brought her here in the first place.

On the surface, the Kincaids and (as far as she could ascertain) the St. Johns—all under one roof—were making an effort to be hospitable.

But, in the luxury of their home and amid their appraising glances, True was uncomfortable among these wealthy people. She was an alien, a foreigner—not ready or willing to be a cousin. She belonged in the picture she was about to hand Michael's Cousin Emily. But, first her grandfather. . . .

"Is this the man you knew?" True asked, handing the photograph to Emily.

Emily's eyes lighted up, making words unnecessary as she studied the dark, good looks of the then-youthful man. At length she spoke.

"Jimmy," she said. And then the woman added something almost inaudible. Surely True's ears deceived her. *Could* Emily Kincaid have said, "*My* Jimmy?"

"I never heard him called by that name," True said. "You're sure—"

Emily stiffened.

"I'm very sure. How could I have forgotten? Had your grandmother not come to spend that fateful summer . . . or even if we had played a different game! I will never believe she did not know Jimmy was behind the door when girls guessed the identity," Emily colored, "and discreet young ladies guessed wrong purposely—lest they be—oh, this is indelicate!—*kissed,* and in this very house."

In spite of herself, True giggled. Her hostess did not join her, and True sighed inwardly. That stolen kiss, planned or otherwise, very well may have been the only one exchanged in this place.

Well, this woman's love affairs, or lack of them, had nothing to do with her. It was good, however, that she knew something of the Kelly family—

Emily broke into her thoughts.

"Fine family, the Kellys. Fine, indeed, regular bluebloods like the Kincaids and St. Johns. And background is *so* important—essential when choosing one's mate, since it ties together two families forever."

True did not meet Emily's eyes. She had a strong feeling that there was more behind her words than the long-ago romance which never blossomed. It was a relief when the other woman asked to see the other photograph True held.

"Maybe you will remember the daughters—"

"Jimmy, my personal name for him, only had one."

In the short silence, True could hear the pounding of her heart. This was thin ice.

"Yes," she said, choosing her words carefully, "but my—I mean, when the man you call Jimmy Kelly was killed, his wife remarried."

"My dear young woman," Emily Kincaid said crisply, "I do not need you to jog my memory."

Rebuffed, True was on the verge of snatching the picture, thanking her hostess for her questionable hospitality, and ordering a carriage. But then Emily was speaking normally again, as if nothing had happened.

"Jimmy's widow let no grass grow on his grave after the explosion before finding herself another mate! And, as for that Stein man . . . but, wait, am I speaking of your grandfather? There *was* another daughter. Ah, yes, here she is—Mary

Evangeline, wasn't it? Exactly like her mother, face of an angel—but who knows what evil lurks in the heart?"

There was a wild desire to run at this woman. Tear at the delicate skin. Break down this regal shell.

But it would defeat the cause. And nothing would touch her anyhow.

Caution. I must use caution. Over and over she told herself that.

True realized that Emily was speaking. Hoping she had missed none of the words, she listened carefully.

"—She left here, of course, and in disgrace, I might add. Rumor had it that she got into trouble with some Eastern man. Could have been anybody, of course. You never can tell about women like that. Once they go bad, there's no changing them—"

"Oh, I don't agree! I don't agree at all—"

"You know nothing of such women. They may delude themselves into thinking they'll make their hearts right, but the road to hell's paved with good intentions. Made by evil people . . . but why are we speaking of someone you never knew? Although, I must say, you inherited your aunt's dangerous physical features. Sad, indeed, that you didn't take after your mother. Odd, isn't it, that your mother looks so like her father and that blonde gene continues to travel through the generations! Now Christen Elizabeth, your mother, was different in every way.

Speak up, True. Speak up now. Correct this deception. But the tongue that could have told the truth clove to the roof of her mouth.

Was she afraid of this woman or was she trying to gather information she could not have gleaned as the "bastard child of the wayward Mary Evangeline Stein?"

Part of both, she decided with the only corner of her brain that was able to think in the cloud of confusion. But of one thing she was certain. She, True North, was not ashamed of her heritage. She was proud of her family. Never mind blue blood!

Overcome with an overwhelming desire to get out of this house, True reached for the photograph.

But Emily drew back.

"The rest of these people—who are they, True?"

"It's hard to explain. No, easy to explain, but hard to understand. They really have nothing to do with—"

"If they are descendants of Jimmy's, they concern me!" Emily's voice carried an edge.

It was hard to imagine why. But, then, everything about this situation was unimaginable. So why not get it over with? And quickly!

"Part of us are his descendants," True said, choosing her words carefully. "It will be easier if I use full names—if that is all right?" *Safer, too. . . .*

Emily nodded in agreement.

"I'll know the relationship."

True studied the photograph. How well she remembered the day the traveling photographer came to Turn-Around Inn, an unforgettable Easter Sunday.

Swallowing the lump in her throat, True began, "This is Christen Elizabeth Kelly, as you know—"

"Your mother."

No, my aunt! Should she say it? Quickly True went on.

"The man to her left is Joseph Craig, a wonderful minister. And between Christen Elizabeth and Mary Evangeline is Dr. Wilson North. The tall, dark boy holding me is Young Wil, Dr. North's nephew. The boy my age, holding Young Wil's hand, is Marty. Marty's parents died in a flood and the Craigs took him in—"

"In a sense, then, Marty is your brother?"

In a sense, yes, but not the way you think. You have identified the wrong young woman as my mother. True realized then that there was no way she could tell of Angel Mother's death, followed by Uncle Joe's—and the subsequent marriage of Aunt Chrissy to Daddy Wil.

Well, that did make Marty her brother . . . better let it go at that.

She was about to replace the photograph in

her bag when Emily Kincaid's shrewd eyes focused on her, compelling her to look up. Dark, young eyes locked with faded blue ones and the gazes held. Even before the question came, True—careful as she had been—knew that it would concern something she had touched upon quickly if at all.

"Am I to gather then that the wayward Mary Elizabeth came to that wild frontier to give birth to that—that—"

"Baby," True supplied. Emily Kincaid did not know her well enough to detect the dangerous quiet of the voice.

"Her baby was born dead, then?"

"Mary Evangeline lost one child, yes," True said, remembering the painful account of her mother's trying to bear a child to her beloved Wilson.

It was something that this unfeeling woman would be unable to understand—an unselfish act of love. Angel Mother had known the risks . . . even then had been in fragile health . . . but nothing mattered except her love, which could never die, no matter what happened to her flesh.

So let the woman think the lost child was True herself.

"It has nothing to do with us, Miss—"

"Cousin Emily," the woman corrected. "Michael should be home tomorrow, as I am sure you are aware, and we must have another long talk—this time about our own relationship."

No, she did *not* know when Michael was returning. And there *was* no relationship. Whatever was going on here had to be corrected. And at once! She was glad, for that reason, that Michael St. John was coming home so soon.

True glanced at the grandfather clock at the far end of the great bedroom.

"My!" she said, "I had no idea it was so late. If you will excuse me, I must get dressed."

Emily rose to stand her full height. Did she never make an ungraceful gesture?

"Yes, you will wish to see the ruins of your home. I will accompany you—"

True swung a foot onto the carpeted floor.

"No, please—this is something I must do alone. Also, I must mail an important letter and locate a telegraph office to let my family know I am all right."

"I will order the carriage," Emily said as she turned to leave. "It is good that we got to know each other better."

Only we don't! True's heart protested. *It's a case of mistaken identity . . . one I may NEVER be able to correct. . . .*

12

Magnolia Manor

Once she had sent Aunt Chrissy and Daddy Wil word that she was safe, True felt a sense of relief. The night letter would arrive the following day, the telegrapher said.

She only wished her bulky letter to Young Wil would go through as fast. Miss Emily had said it was perfectly all right to receive mail at the Kincaid-St. John mansion, so True had given the address without explanation.

It would be wonderful to hear from Young Wil again. Actually, she understood very little of what he told her concerning his studies in pathology. But she clung to his every word, honored that he would choose her as the one in whom he confided. At those times they were very close. Young Wil didn't tease about the two freckles on her nose. And he did not treat her like a child!

Remembering their countless tramps through the Oregon forests, forever in search of new forms of plant life for Young Wil's botany courses or animal fossils for zoology, True wished that he were with her now. Young Wil knew how to turn everything into an adventure—and how to make her feel safe and cared for at the same time.

Maybe, she thought slowly for the first time, it was better to be thought of as young and inexperienced than pushed into the foreign role of maturity. Especially when one had to cope alone. . . .

A brisk breeze had risen. Autumn leaves pattered down noiselessly at her feet. True realized then that she had been so engrossed in her thoughts that she surely must have passed the home where her mother and aunt grew up.

The section of the city that she had entered was in shambles. Here and there a few stone fireplaces, once a part of the great houses they had warmed, stood as if waiting for their owners to return. Rotting foundations, barely visible through the tangle of brambles, marked where other mansions had stood.

Some of the places, she saw, were posted with NO TRESPASSING signs. Nobody seemed to have bothered with the others. Nothing here resembled the Kelly home.

She was about to turn when she spotted the lonely-looking figure of an elderly black man. Sitting on the edge of what had once been a wishing well, the man appeared to be dozing. In his hand was a pair of shears.

True cleared her throat. Startled, the man sprang to his feet. She saw then that he was even older than she had supposed.

" 'Scuse me, missy—I don't mean no harm bein' here abouts. Lemme git from yore way—"

And like a frightened rabbit, the old fellow stepped aside for True to pass through the gate. He had removed the ragged straw hat to reveal a head of frizzled, cotton-white hair which he now held in his hands.

"I jest come heah t'wish—"

"It's quite all right," True said quickly. "And you needn't be afraid. I don't belong here either. I'm looking for a house and I thought perhaps you could direct me." She handed him a slip of paper carrying the address.

The man shook his head sorrowfully without looking up.

"I cain't read th' words," he murmured.

Compassion filled True's heart. Feeling as embarrassed as the man looked, she was about to thank him and move on when the ebony face brightened.

"Did she have uh name—th' house? Mostly, they did, I recollects."

Of course! She should have thought of that.

"Magnolia Manor," True replied.

Dropping the shears, the man forgot his shyness and raised a pair of dark and shining eyes.

"I knowed it," he whispered in a near-croon. "I tole my Mandy afore she went to be wid th' Lawd that someday one o'you-all wuz shure t'come home."

It was True's turn to be taken aback.

"You mean—you mean, *this* is it? This is all that's left of Magnolia Manor?"

"The' buildin's all went blazin—and th' lootin' follawed no mattah how hard us colored folks tried t'save th' only home we evah had. But th' trees is heah—'member them mossy oaks wheah you-all and yo big sistah used to swing? Allus wantin' I should swing you highah than yo mammy thunk was safe." His laugh was mellow with recollection of another generation.

"How wonderful that I've found you," True said warmly. "And forgive me for not introducing myself. I am True North. What is your name?"

"Name's Joshua—and I allus added Kelly on, secretlike." The man scratched his head in confusion. "But the name ain't right fer you-all. I got no book larnin', but I got myself a memory—Miss Vangie, we all said, Miss Vangie, our Li'l White Chile!"

True moved over to take the gnarled, black hand in hers.

"You're close, Joshua—very close. I'm her daughter."

A look of sheer joy crossed the weathered face, and he favored her with a toothless grin.

"Don't mattah none. You-all'l wan' the' yawd puttin' shape 'fore the buildin' starts. Best I be workin', Miss—"

"Just True, please, Joshua." True inhaled deeply, wondering what to say next. But he mustn't be allowed to count on something which would never materialize.

"Let's hold off on any more work—at least for now. Agreed?"

For a moment the old man looked disappointed. Then his countenance brightened.

"Ain't no rush. Nobody's to bothah us none, 'ceptin' maybe th' feller from the courthouse."

"What fellow, Joshua? Someone you know?"

Joshua shook his grizzled head.

"Lawman mebbe—sumpin' 'bout railroad bizness fer Miss Vangie."

13

Homecoming

There was so much that True would have asked of the old gardener if there had been time. Later she was to regret hurrying away, for the two of them were never to meet again.

But Emily Kincaid had said that dinner would be early this evening, and her request that all gather in the library by six o'clock was a command.

One simply did not cross the woman, True thought a little resentfully, as she hurried away from the ruins of her mother's childhood home and the only living person, as far as she knew, who might have helped her put together the missing pieces that her mother's diary had omitted.

Buried in her thoughts, True was at first unaware that somebody or something stood before her. And then she realized that Michael St. John had appeared from nowhere like an apparition.

"I know I should have waited at the house," he said apologetically, taking another step toward her, "but I could not wait to see if I was right—without an audience!"

He looked at True with hazel eyes which in

the slanted rays of the setting sun looked bright and innocent. A little smile of appreciation played about the corners of his mouth above the carefully trimmed beard.

Feeling a mixture of emotions she was unable to identify, True could only murmur, "Right? Right about what?"

Even as she waited for Michael's answer, she felt herself smiling in return. Here was a friend in what she could only assume was enemy territory, although the "why" of either was yet a mystery—one he could help resolve.

"Right about your beauty, my dear. And you may rest assured that is not intended as idle flattery. Through those dull meetings I kept seeing that special golden look of yours. 'But, Michael,' I said, 'no young lady's hair can outshine the moon. No pair of eyes can change from sky blue to royal purple—and no face can be shaped like a delicate cameo—' "

At the word *cameo*, he stopped short. And True felt her own quick intake of breath. Automatically her hand flew to her throat, pausing at the spot where she ordinarily wore the pearl-and-sapphire brooch.

As important a part as the precious heirloom had played in the lives of her mother, her aunt, and herself, how *could* she, even in this strange new world, have forgotten until this moment that she had been forced to surrender it in the holdup or be taken hostage?

The sunset glow turned to a peculiar white haze. The cobblestone street was rising up to meet her. And the moss-bearded oak trees were dancing about her in a dizzying quadrille. . . .

Through it all she was only dimly aware that Michael reached out to steady her and then gathered her into his arms. She clung to him as one clings to a lifeline. Caught in a riptide of emotions, Michael was solid ground.

Not thinking of his arms as an embrace, True relaxed against the smoothness of his vest and let her eyes droop closed.

Michael was speaking, but she paid no attention to the words—just their tone, which was smooth velvet. Soothing her. Making her long to sleep.

Was it possible to go to sleep standing up? *Surely she must be dreaming,* True thought. Dreaming the words she heard. And surely sleep accounted for her feeling of helplessness. Weightlessness. Her total levity. What was the handsome, sandy-haired man in her dreams saying?

"Rest, my darling—that's it, rest. They've worn you out. I should have known it would be too much. Rest, my Sleeping Beauty, and when you awaken, there is much—so much—we must talk about. A lifetime of planning—but for now, *rest.*"

And when she would have opened her eyes,

he kissed them closed. *Darling,* he'd called her . . . the wrong man . . .

Later True wondered how long the two of them stood there beneath the oaks. She began to regain consciousness when the gathering evening breeze swept the Evangeline moss against her face; and then—not satisfied—wrapped itself about them as if to bind them together.

When she opened her eyes, the sun was down and there was a strange, yellow glow where the sun had been. How could she have let this happen?

"Oh, Michael—we must go," she murmured hastily. "Miss Kincaid, your Cousin Emily, doesn't like to be kept waiting!"

Reluctantly, he released her. Then, with a little laugh, he reached for her hand and tucked it beneath his arm.

"I see she got to you, all right. Was the meeting very awful?"

Matching her steps to his, True tried to appraise the situation.

"Not awful, I guess," she said slowly—"more frightening. I'm sure none of them like me—but, then, why should they? Oh, I'm not making sense at all!"

They were nearing the mansion. It looked even more ominous in the shadows than by daylight.

True had had a feeling of foreboding earlier. Now the feeling was worse—as if the night moths which were beginning to fill the air around them were loosed inside her as well.

The mansion was so tall. So dark, except for the windows—all angrily ablaze at their tardiness—which seemed to watch their every move as True and Michael moved up the narrow path left by the heavy growth of hedge.

The veranda, she saw now, wrapped both sides of the great house. Bay windows jutted out at every corner and, in spite of the vine-draped pillars, something about the recent architecture changed the plantation-period house from a colonial mansion to a Victorian castle.

Maybe it was the round tower on the back roof, shaped like a witch's hat. Involuntarily she shuddered, realizing what was wrong with the house. It lacked love.

Michael lowered his voice.

"You make all the sense in the world, my dear. Meeting them, especially Cousin Emily, can be a fiasco. She's our self-appointed guardian of the family fortune." He chuckled. "And the family's good name, I might add."

True drew back.

"And she thought I had designs on you? Is that why she was so remote and—well, cautious? Oh, Michael, I never should have accepted your hospitality. I had no right . . . but, tell me, how could she have suspected such?"

Pulling her behind a giant magnolia, as if to

hide from the staring windows, Michael gripped both her hands.

"I accept full responsibility for that impression, True. I wanted you to be cared for—looked after—until I could get here to do it. And it was necessary that I imply that we—well, had an arrangement."

True tried to pull away.

"I feel used somehow," she whispered. "Used and rebuffed—and, yet, guilty, because I let it happen."

She felt on the verge of tears.

Michael's voice was low and pleading, something which surprised her about the caustic man with all his polished social graces.

"Wrong on all three counts, my dear—*wrong!* You must believe that. Oh, we should have talked before the gathering of the clan. My intentions are strictly honorable—and you have not led me on. I want to make you mine—"

"*Michael!* Is that you in the garden?" Emily Kincaid's voice, though pleasant, carried an edge which sliced through the balmy night air.

Anticipating her inward rage, True shuddered again. Her hostess would be wearing an elegant gown, her neck encased in pearls, while she herself was rumpled and untidy.

There would scarcely be time to wash up before joining the clan of (she hoped the Lord would forgive the word) *vultures* in the library.

Ducking in (a bit ungracefully, she feared),

True made a flying trip to her room. Pouring water into the china basin, she recalled that she had told Michael nothing of the robbery. Neither had she thanked him for use of his quarters.

He was right. They *must* talk. . . .

14

On Trial

"Dinnah is surved, Miz Emily."

With Hosea's softly spoken announcement, Emily Kincaid rose in signal for the others to rise also. Oscar escorted the hostess through the dining room arch. Michael politely waited for all the others (whose names and relationships True was still unable to identify) to follow.

Then, with a slight twinkle in his eye, he offered her his arm. Gratefully she took it. Whatever else Michael St. John might or might not be, he was a gallant, "a gentleman of fine breeding," she supposed they would phrase it here.

How could he have failed to see how she stood out—in a wrong way—in her tailored navy suit, simple, high-necked blouse adorned only with a single-strand pearl necklace, while the other women were bustled and ruffled as if for a gala party?

He himself was dressed so impeccably —everything about him giving off an aura of fastidiousness—that he had to be comparing her unfavorably. If so, he gave no sign of it. That gave True confidence to get through the grueling evening which was to follow.

She wished he had warned her what to expect, but he probably knew no other world himself.

Tisha brought turtle soup. Did True like turtle soup? Emily inquired. True didn't know. Then Tisha was pleased to have the finger bowls ready for Miss North in case she did not care for the flavor.

The maid stood ready with the fragile, cut-glass bowl on which rose petals floated. Small talk went on around her. But True had the feeling that all eyes were focused on her as she lifted the soup spoon and, careful to dip away from her, touched the creamed, green liquid to her lips.

Why were they all staring? The soup was flat and tasteless, since she was in no condition for her taste buds to work.

But if it had been made of green persimmons, she would have gone on with the silly game they were playing. So she forced a smile.

"Isn't True all I told you she was?" Michael's voice, laced with pride, broke into True's consciousness.

Emily Kincaid laid down her spoon and rang the silver bell beside her.

"I'm sure she is, Michael—and much more."

The small addendum was not lost on True.

Please, Michael, she willed. *Please say no more—*

"Has she told you that some of her ancestry goes back to Boston?"

"You may bring the salad, Hosea," Emily instructed. Then she turned to True. "How interesting, my dear! An old established family?"

"Boston-Irish," True remembered Aunt Chrissy's calling the Blake family.

Then, in an effort to lighten the moment, "But I doubt if they were able to crowd into the *Mayflower*. Surely it must have been overloaded!"

There was no laughter. Michael saved the moment by reaching out to place a steadying hand on hers.

"I kept True a secret, Cousin Emily, in the hope that I could be here for the trial! Does she pass the test?" Light words, but meaningful.

True colored under Emily's scrutiny. The older woman was comparing her, of course, to the other women in the room . . . the other women in Michael's life . . . and some Southern belle she had chosen for her cousin as a suitable wife.

Well, it was best to get the whole thing out in the open. Let them know that she was here for the exact reasons she had mentioned. Her stay in the city would be brief. And it would not be here in this house!

Where should she begin? With her mother's secret—or the fact that she had never eaten turtle soup before.

Before she could think of appropriate words, Emily spoke again.

"I regret that you were late this evening—"

"We've apologized." True was unable to hold her tongue.

As if she had not spoken, Emily continued, "We were to make some plans regarding your introduction to our circle of friends. As soon as your trunks arrive."

And have something suitable to wear. They were ashamed of her. Tears sprang to her eyes. She did not belong in their shallow, glittering world. She felt on the very top of a high cliff about to topple into a canyon below.

How silly of her to feel that way! All she had to do was walk out! Why, then, did she feel trapped?

True gripped Michael's hand, hoping it would signal her desire to escape. The tightened fingers brought a look of pleased surprise; but, before she could convey a further message, Emily spoke over his head.

"Tell me, my dear, did you find what you were looking for this afternoon—yes, you may removed the plates and bring the main course, Tisha. Did you not like the salad, True?"

True looked at her untouched plate, aware of the salad's presence for the first time.

"I—I'm sorry—I seem to have little appetite—"

"All the excitement has been trying. I should have gone with you uninvited this afternoon. Tell me, was that eccentric colored man there again? He rambles on so foolishly—"

True answered briefly. She was reluctantly to talk about the afternoon, or, for that matter, herself. But, yes, a nice man who called himself Joshua was there, she said.

Emily leaned forward, her face strained. And around her True felt the raised eyebrows of over a dozen members of this family up and down the table.

"Did he make mention—"

So that's it! They want to know about the "feller from the courthouse." But why?

And then Michael exploded a cannon.

"Let's not exhaust True. Bear in mind that she has not said, 'Yes' to me yet."

15

I Want to Go Home, Lord!

After the tense dinner hour, True pleaded a headache and escaped to her room.

"Please don't linger, Michael," she begged. "There is so much we must discuss—I'm so confused—so bewildered—but not tonight. I have to be alone!"

Later she wondered if she had been rude. Certainly she had all but shut the door in Michael's face. And he had done nothing to deserve that . . . or had he?

Who was responsible for this mess, anyway? And how had she veered so far off her course? Or maybe she hadn't. Everything was so shrouded in mystery. . . .

Too excited to think clearly, True turned up the wick on the gas lamp beside her bed and read Uncle Joe's Bible. But the words ran together and she did not find the usual comfort in the Scriptures.

Michael's face kept drifting between her and the pages, his hazel eyes sometimes admiring, sometimes quizzical, and sometimes frighteningly shrewd.

When the shrewd expression came, True

squeezed her own eyes closed to shut out the part of him that bothered her.

And then the face wasn't Michael's. It was Young Wils—so real that she felt she could reach out and touch him, push the boyhood cowlick away from his broad forehead so she could look into the dark, thoughtful eyes that could turn roguish and back to pensive without notice.

A carbon copy of Daddy Wil, his frame was a little taller, a little more powerful than his uncle's—which accounted for his looking equally at home in lumberjack garb of the Northwest or his Sunday best.

Oh, how she missed him! Given the opportunity, she would put up with his teasing—even welcome it! How long did it take a letter to reach Portland, anyway?

Better yet, maybe she would be finished here before his answer came . . . or the Lord's. . . .

With that thought, True sat straight up in bed. What was it she had said? That Atlanta might be home, after all? Or maybe even Boston?

It occurred to her suddenly that she had not had a heart-to-heart talk with the Lord for too long.

Quickly sliding from between the linen sheets, she knelt beside the bed. Then, tucking her long nightgown about her chilled feet, True poured her heart out to God.

"Why is it, Lord, that I forget You even when I know You never forget me? Forgive my neglect.

Forgive my disloyalty to You—and maybe to my wonderful family—although You know I never intended that. . . ."

And then the tears came as she prayed for each of her loved ones by name: "Daddy Wil, Aunt Chrissy, Young Wil, the twins, and Marty —wherever he is—"

True stopped at that point, aware that something she was unable to pinpoint bothered her. When no insight came, she continued.

The great clock by the window seat interrupted her rudely.

"Funny thing about clocks," Young Wil had said once, "they fold their hands but can't learn to keep quiet even during our family prayers!"

Family prayers . . . that was something else amiss in this house. Nobody prayed. At least not aloud.

Seemingly satisfied with its 12 strokes, the clock was silent and True finished her prayer.

"I need Your guidance, Lord. I really don't know who I am or where I belong. I had hoped this visit would teach me—but I am only more confused. Lead me home—wherever home is. Right now I want to go where I *think* I belong. But something is holding me back. . . ."

• • •

The time that followed was a confusion of people, each—it seemed to True—with a hidden motive, each different.

She had resolved to have a private talk with Michael. It was imperative, to save further embarrassment and possible heartbreak, that they come to an understanding. He had given the impression that theirs was a friendship of long standing—*more* than a friendship, actually, something this clan seemed to have sunk their collective teeth into. Surely that was why Emily Kincaid had put her through the third degree.

Well, she thought with a glow of pride, *nobody could say she was not of gentle breeding!* Aunt Chrissy had seen to that. And, although Daddy Wil's income as a country doctor was small and she herself had left just as she was to the age of helping out, True had felt that her mode of dress was well above the average afforded other girls her age in the Oregon settlement.

Willowy-thin, her regal bearing compensated when she had to make do with a new scarf or flower in place of a new gown. Until now!

Now everything about her was wrong . . . but was it only the clothes? There was the matter of background. Well, there again, she had nothing of which to be ashamed!

Aware then that she was on the defensive, True pushed the unworthy ideas aside. After all, she reminded herself again, she was a guest here—until she could get around to her second resolution, which was to find a place to stay until she had checked out a few other details concerning her past . . . and something else.

What was causing the vague uneasiness? In a sense these people had been hospitable—maybe in the only way that "monied people" knew how to be.

Were they always suspicious of newcomers? Or was she a special kind of interloper? The uneasiness went deeper. It had to do with Magnolia Manor.

Sometime she must get around to seeing how to check on her losses in the robbery, some facts of which still puzzled her. . . .

Had any girl ever been confronted with more? Yes, of course! Her mother and aunt had been in much worse circumstances . . . *only they had escaped by running away.*

Well, she wasn't going to run! Whatever was wrong here, she would stay and fight it to the finish. Her rounded chin jutted out as she decided that the first priority was to have the talk with Michael St. John.

But it was slow in coming. True desperately needed to get her simple wardrobe in order. She asked Tisha about an ironing board and almost regretted it, so great was the young girl's reaction to the question.

"I's so sorry, Miz True. I shudda dun yo things."

"We'll work together, Tisha," True offered, which seemed to frighten the girl all the more.

In the end, Tisha allowed her to take the garments away one by one to be aired and pressed as she removed them from the suitcases.

The clothes were still wrong. But True felt a little more at ease once they looked smoothed free of wrinkles. And fortunately there was a lot she could do with her hair. Flowers seemed to be in eternal bloom here, and a camellia pinned to the crown of her long hair was most becoming.

Or so were her thoughts as she went down to the evening meal on Saturday.

Michael had been out riding "over the plantation," according to Tisha. And so she saw him for the first time as they met with the usual ritualistic formality in the library.

"Charming, my dear." His voice had a ring of sincerity.

There was an exchange of small talk, the grand march into the dining room, and then Emily's announcement: "We will all be attending church tomorrow morning. Tell me, True, are there any organized churches on the frontier?"

Angry words rose to True's lips, but she put them aside. Churning inwardly, but outwardly calm, she answered simply, "Many of them."

She was about to add that her uncle had been a dedicated minister, but thought better of it. Certainly she had no desire to get into family relationships again.

"And do you attend?"

Emily Kincaid's question caused True to

106

choke on the bite of fillet-of-sole mousse she was supposed to be enjoying. Reaching for her water goblet, she all but tipped it over.

The other woman did not seem to notice.

"I mean, with all those savages around—well, I would think any public gathering would be unsafe. Does one dare wear her jewelry?"

Praying for strength, True took a sip of water from her glass. What did this family want of her, anyway?

"I hardly know how to answer your questions." True realized that her voice was cold, but suddenly it did not matter.

"Yes, I attend church. And we do not refer to the Indians as 'savages.' As a matter of fact," she felt her voice rising, "we do not consider Oregon a 'frontier' anymore. We are quite civilized! As to the jewels, I have very few, as I am sure you have observed."

True paused, not so much for breath as to let the full implication of her words soak in and let Emily Kincaid see that she, "the homespun frontier woman," was not blind.

When she resumed, her words opened a new topic—one she felt needed further discussion.

"As a matter of fact, it was in these environs—not in the Oregon Country—that I was robbed of a very precious piece of jewelry."

Emily Kincaid was not enjoying the turn of the conversation, as evidenced by the high spots of color in her cheeks. But nobody was going to break through her facade of affected poise.

"And we must be looking into recovering the brooch for True, Michael. I will get in touch with Inspector Devore Monday. He will wish to speak with True . . . and now about church tomorrow, have you suitable clothes, True?"

"Really, Cousin Emily, I feel that could be offensive." Michael's voice was low, almost a growl.

"Why, I meant nothing at all—except to offer a light wrap in case there is an autumn chill. Her trunks have not arrived—"

True laid down her fork.

"Would you mind terribly if Michael and I skipped dessert?" Could that deadly voice be hers? "I have lost my appetite and there is some talking Michael and I need to do—in case," she added with a growing acidity, "the outside air is no chillier than this—"

Rising, she stood her full height. Let her chair tilt backward. Let her water glass upset and splash water the full length of the formal lace tablecloth. Let Michael remain seated. Whatever! *She* was going to escape. And now.

None of it happened, of course. Michael was behind her chair in one swift, fluid motion. And together they left the startled diners.

Home? *This?* It never could be. . . .

• • •

The outdoor air was sweet with night-blooming cerus. Somewhere in the gathering darkness a cicada, reluctant to let go of summer, chirped for a mate. In the light of a half-moon, Michael's eyes turned from hazel to coffee, True noted dully. Coffee with cream, the moonlight adding mellifluous tones.

He was a part of the setting—unreal. Reality lay back home in Oregon, and she must escape this strange land, else she would become a part of the unreality.

It was unreal, too, that Michael's arms were reaching out and she was walking into them for comfort.

"I have to get away, Michael." Her voice was dead of emotion.

"True, listen to me, dear one." Michael withdrew one of his arms to cup her chin in his hand and bring her eyes to meet his. "They are not as bad as they seem. There's a lot of stiff-necked pride—and money—"

"I never would have guessed," she murmured, but she could feel blood flowing through her being again.

"And, of course, Cousin Emily pulls the strings. The others are puppet-heirs."

"I wouldn't have guessed that either!"

Michael laughed.

"Ouch! Do I fall into that category, too, True? Your answer is important. *Very* important."

True inhaled deeply.

"I don't know Michael. I honestly don't know what I feel about you. There has been so little time. And everything has moved so fast that it seems like a dream. One doesn't think in a dream."

"Love requires no thinking. It's a matter of the heart."

True's heart skipped a beat.

"We weren't talking about love, Michael—"

"But we *have* to talk about it! Isn't that one of the main topics we need to discuss?"

When Michael would have tightened the circle of his arms about her, True ducked playfully from reach and laughed. A few minutes earlier her spirits had plummeted. She was a frump. A nothing-at-all.

Now, unexplainably, she felt better. And the laugh she managed was light.

Michael responded to her mood. Twirling his sandy mustache in mock-villainry, he said, "Ah, me proud beauty, so it pleases you to play hard to get! But it is I who will pay the rent."

The words, so playfully spoken, brought True back to the problems at hand.

"Oh, Michael, what am I going to do?"

"Why, you're going to marry me, of course! There has been no doubt in my mind since I first laid eyes on you. And get it out of your pretty head that my feelings have anything to do with background or money. I hoped you would like the family and I know they will accept you—"

110

True felt the beginnings of another headache.

"They don't have to *accept* me, Michael! I'm not staying on. Why should I?"

"As my wife!"

The headache materialized.

"Nothing's decided," she whispered. "Nothing at all. I have to go on to Boston . . . and there's Magnolia Manor . . . I need to see who owns it—"

"You do." Michael's answer was immediate.

"I'm not sure—"

"About an answer to my proposal or who owns that piece of property? I know the answer to both! And, incidentally, there's land that goes with the house—quite a large parcel. Rundown, of course, but land all the same and maybe valuable sometime."

Land? No, she hadn't known. She wasn't sure it even mattered. *And,* she thought foggily, *who would be entitled to the property? Originally it was the Kelly home and would have been Aunt Chrissy's. But when Grandmother married my grandfather . . .*

"Why the frown? A moment ago you seemed almost happy." Michael's voice carried a note of concern.

"I was thinking, for one thing, that we've been discussing family and seeming to get nowhere. And in all this time I have not met your father."

Michael's face became sober.

"Don't think I've forgotten that! But I have been waiting for the right time. Father has his good days and his bad. He has suffered almost total paralysis and has lost some of the power of speech. He occupies the upstairs east wing of the house—owns the house, incidentally, and 50 percent of the railroad shares—that is, among the owners we know about. One is missing."

He frowned and looked away.

16

A Week of Revelations

The week that followed was the strangest of True North's life. Later she was to look back on it as a week of revelations. . . .

Sunday.

The day dawned bright and clear. "Shirt-sleeve weather," O'Higgin would have said. No need for a wrap.

True dressed in her dark blue suit and added a face-veil to her flat-top hat. The other women of the house wore fur-trimmed suits.

Maybe she should have brought along a shawl just for appearance—an idea she shrugged off. She was unaccustomed to people who did things for appearance sake and she wasn't sure she liked them very well.

Emily Kincaid kept her distance as the group waited for the carriage to be brought to the front of the mansion. The woman had been coolly polite, nothing more, since True had spoken her piece—which suited True fine.

One more mention of the "overdue trunks" and True was going to tell her there were going to *be* no trunks. And just maybe, she thought spiritedly, she might add a few more tidbits about herself that would prove as shocking for this overpowering woman.

But when Emily spoke, her words were addressed to Michael.

"It was good of you to come along, seeing that you attend only Easter and Christmas services—or some other special occasion."

"This *is* a special occasion," Michael replied. If he planned to explain, there was no opportunity. The carriage had arrived.

Carriage? No, a Cinderella's coach! True stared in disbelief at the cut-under body style of the fringe-topped surrey, constructed of hardwood and steel, carpeted in red velvet. And the seats—weren't they upholstered in genuine leather? And in white! How long could white hold up?

"May I help you, True?" Michael's voice broke into her reverie.

True, suddenly aware that she had been gaping, clamped her mouth shut and lifted her skirts slightly in preparation to stepping up to the wide step and into the "pumpkin coach."

Seated between Michael and Oscar, True continued to look around her in admiration.

"How beautiful!" she exclaimed, seeing the oil-burning lanterns on either side of the carriage. "Daddy Wil has to hang a lantern in front of his old buggy when he makes an emergency night call. Maybe Young Wil can—"

Aware that she was thinking aloud, True

stopped in mid-thought. A flush of embarrassment stained her cheeks.

Oscar was talking over his shoulder to the red-
haired cousin—Audrey Anne, wasn't that her
name? The others were listening to him so that
only Michael heard True's words.

"That makes a good dozen times you've spoken of him," he said softly. "What is he to you?"

What was he to her? True gulped and tried to
smile. Then she swallowed and tried again. But
it was no use. Her chest was tight. Her throat
hurt. And there were tears burning behind her
eyeballs at the mention of his name.

Strive as she would, True was sure that her
imitation of a human voice was not creditable.

"Why, he's—Young Wil's my—uh,
cousin—well, stepbrother—no, none of those—not
really. I mean he's my friend, the one who helped
bring me up."

The glance she turned to Michael would have
to plead for understanding. Certainly she had no
words to cover the relationship.

"Does that clear things up?"

"Oh, perfectly!" Michael's laugh was as low
as his words. He reached out to touch her hand.
"It tells me nothing, except what I really wanted
to know—that this fellow's the rival I've been
asking you about!"

The carriage stopped. A liveried driver helped
the group from the carriage. And, with Emily
Kincaid sweeping grandly ahead, the procession

filed down the aisle to a pew marked "Kincaid-St. John."

Once she was seated in the straight-backed pew, True had a sudden sensation of something indefinable, a sense of *deja vu* that was frightening. She had never seen this place before, and yet every corner was familiar.

The high ceiling would be arched . . . the pulpit draped in gold cloth . . . and there would be a multitude of stained-glass windows darkened by pre-Renaissance art in which the flesh tones were deathly pale, the eyes of the subjects filled with sorrow, and the background shrouded in gray-on-gray to give the illusion of smoke.

Shuddering, True forced herself to look slowly about the shadowy room. When her gaze came to rest on a dismal painting of Moses descending Mount Sinai, his outstretched hands holding the tablet of stone on which the commandments were engraved, she closed her eyes. The picture was too horrible for her mind to accept. For Moses wore a pair of grotesque horns!

It was comforting when Michael reached and covered her white-knuckled hands with his own. But she was unable to thank him with a look because her eyes, when she opened them, were pulled as if by magnet to the scene of horror on the window.

And somehow she knew even before looking that the name below it would be "Stein."

Maybe I never quite believed what they told me,

she thought wildly. *Like Doubting Thomas, I have to feel a nail-scarred hand! But, dear Lord, don't let my faith be like that. . . .*

In that moment, she knew what her mother and aunt had endured.

Then, with closed eyes, she listened to the "hellfire-and-damnation" sermon delivered by an austere man in a long, dark robe. There was no choir and no group singing. And there was no fellowship afterward. True walked out of the church in a state of depression.

"True, I beg your indulgence at this question. But do you really believe like the Reverend Father Holtz?" Michael asked as True was about to go freshen up for Sunday dinner.

"No, Michael," she said simply, "I don't."

"Then why, for heaven's sake, do you put yourself through it?"

Again, she said, "I don't. You see, I grew up knowing a God of love. Does the man ever touch on that subject?"

Michael gave a small laugh.

"Like Cousin Emily said, I don't darken the door very often."

"I can't say I blame you!" Her words surprised him, True thought. And then she added, "But why not give some thought to God's love?"

Michael shrugged and saluted slightly. Which could mean anything . . . giving her more to think about . . . as if she needed more!

· · ·

Monday.

It was one of the senior Mr. St. John's "good days."

"I want you to meet my father, True," Michael said at breakfast. "And, if you don't mind," he said to the rest of the family, "I prefer that the two of us go alone."

A frown creased Emily's face. She erased it quickly.

"Of course," she said abruptly, then to True, "but don't be surprised if his mind wanders—particularly without my presence."

Imagine 36 rooms in this house! True had written to Young Wil in her second letter. This morning she felt that she and Michael passed all 36 rooms before they reached the east-wing suite his father occupied.

Michael opened the door softly, without knocking, and motioned for her to follow him into the quarters. The rooms were full of shadows and a fire flickered sulkily in the grate behind a great four-post bed.

There had been bright sunshine downstairs, she remembered. And then she saw that heavily fringed velvet drapes were drawn against the light of the outside world.

When her eyes adjusted to the semidarkness, True was able to see the features of the man who occupied the oak bed.

118

His face was so wax-like and he lay so still that for a moment she wondered if he was alive. She was about to express concern to Michael when, to her complete surprise, William St. John lifted a feeble white finger and curled it in their direction.

"Come closer." The voice was faint.

Cold with perspiration, True accepted the hand Michael offered and allowed herself to be led to the older man's bedside.

"This is True North, Father. I told you about her—"

"I remember!" The voice held more strength. "Come closer, my dear, so I can see you—my eyes are failing of late."

"Good morning, sir," True said cautiously, hardly knowing what was expected of her. Then, without thinking, she added, "Wouldn't you like the drapes opened a little? It's such a lovely morning!"

At her words, his eyes flew open with a suddenness that startled her. Even in the shadowy room she could see how alike they were—father and son—the same hazel eyes that pierced shrewdly, but not unkindly.

"That voice—it's familiar—come near!"

He was fighting laboriously for breath. Should he be talking? True looked questioningly at Michael. When he nodded, she moved to the bedside and took the feeble, outstretched hand.

"Say something more," Mr. St. John begged, his fingers clinging to hers.

There was something compelling about this man, something True liked instinctively.

"What would you have me say?" she asked lightly, relaxing somewhat.

"The voice—and, yes, even in the darkness, I see the face is the same! Open the drapes a crack, Michael!"

"But Cousin Emily—"

"Drat Cousin Emily! Do as I ask, please."

When a shaft of light appeared in the room, the wan face of the ill man was filled with wonder.

"Mary Evangeline Stein," he said almost reverently.

"You knew her?" True's heart raced with joy. She was about to add, "I am her daughter," when Michael spoke up quickly.

"This is her niece, Father. I understand that the resemblance is quite remarkable. We must not tire you, but I wanted you to know that I have asked this beautiful creature to be my wife—and although as yet I have no answer—"

Had Michael really proposed? Formally? The way a girl expected? Young Wil had always said that love needed a long growing season . . . but she must listen . . . something else was going on in this strange house.

"No answer—never gave me one either—" The voice had grown more feeble already. "Oh, you're beautiful, my dear, so beautiful—and if I had my time to go over—"

Michael signaled to True that it was time to leave, but when she tried to disentangle her fingers from his father's hands, the grip tightened.

"No," he whispered, "don't go . . . I need your promise to use what is yours wisely—your beauty . . . the land . . . and the share of. . . ." The faint voice drifted away and True was able to make out only the word, "Father . . . father. . . ."

"I promise," she said to calm him, having no idea what she was agreeing to. But the faint smile of happiness was enough.

William St. John closed his eyes again and slept. Michael and True tiptoed from the room.

"What was he talking about, Michael? Was he calling for a priest? Or was he speaking of his own father?"

"I don't know," he said. "I'm as puzzled as you—and more than a little surprised that you fitted into the picture. It's all very strange . . . let's not discuss it with Cousin Emily."

"All right," she answered, carefully keeping her eyes on each polished step of the stairs lest he see the immense relief she felt.

Emily Kincaid was the last person on earth with whom she would wish to share *anything!*

• • •

Tuesday.

There was little opportunity to speak with Michael alone; Emily always seemed to be on hand. True had a growing sense of preplanning on the other woman's part.

But in one of her moments with Michael he had made mention of taking her to see the rest of Magnolia Manor on Wednesday. They would take a picnic lunch and have that long overdue talk.

Looking forward to the midweek plan, True caught up on the long letter to Daddy Wil, Aunt Chrissy, and the twins, then started a third letter to Young Wil. She would ask both of them concerning Marty's whereabouts, if they had heard, so she could get in touch with him.

Marty's wandering around and shifting from one job to another was a source of sadness for them all. How long had it been since she had seen him, anyway? Poor Marty! As much as she loved him, True pitied him even more. Not as quick to learn as she and Young Wil, he was at a disadvantage, but she wished he had been less resentful . . . more willing to develop his own potential without feeling threatened by his adopted siblings.

Of course, he *was* easy to ignore, as he said so often . . . easy to forget, too. . . .

Right now she could scarcely remember his face.

Having let her mind wander across the miles that separated True from her family, she was surprised when she was joined by three men, only one of them familiar. One moment she was sitting in the porch swing beneath the wisteria-draped gazebo alone. And the next moment they were there unannounced.

"Sorry, we didn't intend to startle you, Miss North," the man with the familiar face said. "There was no response at the front door—oh, I beg your pardon for not introducing myself. I am Charles Devore, insurance adjuster—"

True accepted his proffered hand.

"I believe we've met," she said slowly.

"No," the man's dark eyes smiled engagingly, "I'd have remembered, I assure you!"

True was unconvinced, so she only half-listened when he introduced the two other men.

Where was it? In spite of his gallant words, she had sensed an uneasiness about him, as if he did not wish to be recognized.

But why? And even after the other two men began asking her questions regarding the train robbery, a part of True's mind kept returning to the identity of the familiar face.

The memory was there. But, like the fragments of a dream, one moment the face was clear and the next moment it was gone. Realizing that she was staring at him in a manner that might be considered rude or even flirtatious, she forced herself to concentrate on the investigation.

How many men came to Mr. St. John's quarters? *Three.*

Description? *One about six feet tall—dark-haired, in need of a haircut. Another, medium height. The third, short.*

Distinguishing marks? *Well, it was dark. And they wore masks. Tall one had a little scar right here,* pointing to her temple. *And there was something about the shortest one's eyes* . . . but there she stopped vaguely.

Something kept her from saying that the eyes, like the face of Investigator Devore, were familiar. Involuntarily she glanced in his direction again, only to find him surveying her, his eyes probing deeply through narrowed lids.

Well, no matter who this man was, he was not one of the bandits. Eyes too dark. Too tall of stature. . . .

Her losses? True described the brooch and, in a choked voice, explained its sentimental value.

A little money, yes, but (she blushed) *not all of it. Some of it was—well, tucked away. . . .*

One of the men whose faces were unfamiliar nudged the other knowingly, at which time Charles Devore stepped back into the picture.

"We will do our best to recover your losses, Miss North—"

"How did you know my name if we've not met?" The question surprised True herself.

"The conductor, of course."

Well, of course. So, synchronized and efficient, the men took turns asking questions and

124

writing down answers. Finally they were finished.

But True was not.

"You should know that the men threatened to take me hostage and that they dealt cruelly with some of the passengers. The conductor and I worked at caring for the injured as best we could—once I was safe—but it was more than a robbery."

Did she imagine it, or was there an exchange of looks between members of the investigating trio?

"Anybody hurt but the coloreds?"

"What possible difference could the color of one's skin have to do with what I'm telling you?" True asked heatedly.

Angered by the attitudes she had seen, she realized too late she took her wrath out on these three. "You know, I get the impression that you're still fighting the Civil War down here—and the South's winning!"

"Anything wrong with that, Miss North?" Devore asked.

"There's plenty wrong with it!" Then, spreading her hands in despair, she said sadly, "Oh, what's the use? Let's get on with this investigation."

The men turned to the door without replying. With his hand on the knob, Charles Devore turned to nod a wordless farewell.

Only it wasn't a farewell. And they both knew

it. He was angry with her and she sensed a vindictiveness within him. As for herself, there would be no rest until she knew . . . but suddenly she did know!

When the door closed, she ran in search of Michael. He was shaking hands with the men at the front gate. When they were gone, she ran to him, white-faced and out of breath.

"True, what is it? What's wrong?" He reached for her limp hand.

"That man," she panted, "the one who calls himself Charles Devore—I know his face, Michael! He's the one I saw through the window the day of the robbery—with the outlaws—a part of them. He *has* to be!"

"Are you sure?" Michael's voice was filled with shock. "He's been in our employ for years—investigates everything concerning our losses. And they were great in the recent robbery."

"Oh, Michael," she whispered. "I'm sure—and being sure makes me afraid!"

• • •

Wednesday.
To her disappointment, True heard a tattoo of raindrops on her window before daybreak. And this was the day for the picnic.

She had hoped that having time alone with Michael would help put recent events into some

126

kind of shape. Each day brought a new set of questions without clearing up the ones of longer standing. What she did not know, as she dressed in the half-light of a gloomy dawn, was that today was to be no exception.

Quickly securing her hair into a coil on top of her head, True picked up a sweater in preparation for going quietly downstairs for coffee. Then she could have her morning's devotionals, continue with her letter-writing, and—time allowing—go back and review her mother's diary.

Time was slipping past rapidly and as yet there had been no opportunity to plan for the trip to Boston. The diary would help prepare her, providing she could settle a few things here . . . find a place to stay, for one thing . . . somewhere reasonable, as money was dwindling. . . .

A soft knock at the door interrupted her thinking.

"Missy True, ma'am—you awake?" It was Tisha! At this hour?

"What is it?" she asked as she fumbled with the lock.

The voice on the other side was low and somewhat anxious.

"Mr. William, he dun wants to be seein' you-all 'fore the others come. Can you come soon-like? Me, I'm takin' coffee—"

But before the girl finished speaking, True had joined her in the hall and locked the door behind her. Together they ascended the stairs sound-lessly, with Tisha looking back frequently.

"Thank you, my dear, for coming!"

Mr. St. John's voice sounded much more clear today. "How lovely you are—and would you do a dying man a favor? Would you pour the way *she* used to?"

"Of course," True smiled. Dismissing Tisha with a nod, she picked up the heavy silver pot. They drank the strong coffee silently while True waited for him to speak.

"There's a box in the highboy there by the closet. Sort of tricky to open."

He explained the combination and asked her to bring it to him. The key was in another com-partment. Would she bring it, too? True did as he asked.

Wondering what all this had to do with her, she watched as the thin fingers of Michael's father struggled with the lock of the box. Some-thing in his manner begged for independence and so she did not offer to help.

The papers inside were yellow and emitted the telltale odor of age.

"You will want to examine these," Mr. St. John said, his voice still strong.

Obediently she accepted the sheath of paper. Old slave ownership papers . . . Confederate money . . . a bundle of letters bound with faded ribbon. Time had dimmed the spidery writing on the documents, and she was unable to make out names or places. Only the block printing remained on legal documents.

"The ownership papers carry a rider on back, freeing slaves who were so vital a part of the plantation."

Why was he telling her this?

"Some here—some at Magnolia Manor."

"But the war—didn't it free them automatically?"

His small laugh was bitter.

"You'd be surprised how many continue to violate—and there's really no enforcement except man's conscience. Hosea, Tisha, and the rest of the staff's ancestors chose to stay. The younger ones are paid—"

When the voice gave way to a cough, True felt a rush of concern. She probably should not be here at all, and certainly she should not allow him to talk.

"You are a kind man, Mr. St. John, but I feel that I am taking your time—intruding, actually—that I should go."

"Stay!" The weak voice carried a command. "These matters concern only you and me."

His mind wandered, Emily had said.

"Really—" True began.

William St. John ignored her interruption.

"The letters are from *her*, your grandmother. You're Chris Beth's daughter? But we both know better, don't we, True?"

Too surprised at the suddenness of the question to think clearly, True was unable to respond.

"Your grandmother, wasn't she? There can be no doubt in my mind that you are that all right. But you are Vangie's child."

There was no question in his voice.

The room was suddenly stifling her. Air. She must have air. Else her lungs would burst.

"Please," she whispered, "please—I must go—what difference could it make? It is past—"

His answer was to extend a large brown envelope taken from the bottom of the box. True accepted it with trembling hands and found herself opening it at his command.

Her eyes refused to focus—as is the way with dreams. And that's what this was—a dream. One from which she could not awake.

"What is it?" Her question came through stiff lips.

"The shares. Railroad shares. There's a third owner, you know. We've looked for years . . . trying to find some trace. Your grandmother came of wealthy stock . . . married Kelly instead of me. . . ."

The voice was failing, but True was powerless now to stop the conversation. She lacked both strength and will.

More. She *must* hear more.

"A family arrangement . . . fragile, like a flower, powerless against them." The piercing eyes turned toward her. "You're like her . . . but different . . . more like a piece of Dresden china that won't let itself be dropped."

The eyes fluttered and closed. Maybe she should terminate the visit. But he had left so much unsaid.

Then to her surprise the determined voice went on, "You are intelligent . . . not going to let Emily, wily as she is, put anything over . . . and I admire your independence . . . Michael will need it." He reached to touch her hand. "You *are* going to marry him?"

"I—I don't know. We—we've reached no agreement. I came here to think—and, well, I think my being here has created a wrong impression. I just can't answer Michael—or you."

"Don't let me press you—it's just that we must draw up the papers while I have the breath . . . so you will be protected. . . ."

"I still don't understand, Mr. St. John."

"Don't be so formal—that pains me deeply when you should have been my daughter . . . or granddaughter—"

"The age difference—what—how?" The words were out before True knew she was going to speak them.

The man's sigh was barely audible above the sounds of the first autumn storm. The rain had stopped, but a blustery wind was tossing leaves against the windows.

"I vowed not to marry after your grandmother broke my heart . . . waiting for her, maybe . . . then, just before she was widowed, I married into the Kincaid family . . . then she married your Grandfather Stein."

The white face twisted in remembered pain. Even now he could not bring himself to speak of the two men who had married her grandmother by their Christian names.

How he must have loved her—loved her the way a woman needs to be loved. Did Michael love her like that? Did he love her at all? Slowly her mind cleared, and she saw something she had failed to see before. Yet how could she have missed it?

"Michael's finding me—it was no accident, was it?" Her whisper seemed to echo in the room.

"No . . . been searching . . . knew you by the picture . . . and by some things you said." The voice broke and was silent like the dying fire in the grate. "Only you are entitled. . . ."

The room had grown chilly—a chill which seeped into her bones and squeezed at her heart.

"Does he know about the circumstances of my birth?" True hardly heard her own words.

The papers lying between them appeared to rise and fall. The beams on the ceiling slanted crazily, and before her very eyes the antique sterling chest seemed to change places with the lowboy from which she had taken the documents tying her into this family. Her mind would no longer function.

"It would make no difference—" William St.

John's hoarse whisper was interrupted by a spasm of coughing. "No difference in the railroad stock . . . belonged to *her* . . . no difference in the inheritance either . . . an attorney this afternoon . . ."

"*Inheritance?*"

"What I choose to leave you . . . go, dear child, before they find you. . . ."

Not sure that her legs would support her, True rose. She should say something. But what? That he had made her feel she belonged here? But that was not true.

With a sinking heart she knew she could never fit into a family who had money to buy anything they wanted—even the respect of others . . . the ones they wanted to cultivate, anyway. . . .

And then it occurred to her that she, True North, was about to fit into the same class. Dully, she wondered whether to feel happy or sad. Like a sleepwalker, she moved to the door.

Then, spinning on her heel, True went back to the bed. No matter how the others behaved, *he* had welcomed her. And for the right reason: love. If not for her, at least for someone in her family. Not for money or background—just love.

Leaning down, she brushed the pale brow with her lips.

"That's for Grandmother," she said softly. And then when she saw the tears flood unashamedly down his cheeks, she repeated the kiss. "And this is for me—Grandfather."

The white face was suddenly a bright sun which lighted the entire room.

"I could die happily now—only I'm not going to! That would please the parasites too much . . . must rest to be ready to see the lawyer . . ." The voice drifted away and then resumed faintly, ". . . must stay . . . don't go away . . . *promise* . . ."

"I promise," True said quickly, seeing that he was no longer able to talk. Only later was she to realize what the commitment would cost her.

• • •

Thursday.
Although True's dreams the night before were a crazy kaleidoscope of seemingly unrelated events, she awakened with an unaccountable sense of excitement. Oh, yes, the picnic!

She needed to get back to Magnolia Manor to find out if it truly belonged to her (and, yes, if she belonged to *it!*).

There was more ground, Michael had said. They would look at it. And, eventually, she would have to make some decisions about it—and a million other things.

But, oh, she thought (stretching luxuriously one leisurely moment before getting dressed), it would be good to get away from problems. To have some time with Michael!

That, of course, accounted for her excitement.

With that thought she was unable to stay in bed to finish the stretch.

Two hours later, with a wicker basket packed with what looked like enough food to last them a week, she and Michael slipped furtively down the stairs.

"Have you ridden a bicycle?" Michael whispered.

True shook her head at the bottom of the stairs.

"I supposed we'd walk."

"With *this?*" He pointed to the basket.

True stifled a giggle.

"Well," she said tentatively, "maybe I can—if it's anything like riding a horse."

"I can't say." His reply was muffled by the sound of a door opening and then closing behind them. "I've never been astride a horse!"

"Such a lot we don't know about each other—" True murmured more to herself than to Michael, who was busy depositing the picnic hamper into a carrier. His next words told her he had heard, however.

"Which is one of the purposes for our day together. Now, let me help you—you'll have no problem, so relax against me. It's a bicycle built for two. Two lovers!"

True laughed self-consciously as she tried to settle herself with some grace onto the unaccustomed seat.

"Lovers," he had said. *Are we lovers?* A thrill

135

prickled her spine and then stopped. *Would Michael love me if he knew?* And then came an even more startling thought: *Would I want him to?*

Her thoughts were interrupted when Michael climbed astride with easy grace and, as he started to pedal slowly, gave True instructions when and when not to pedal. At first she felt 100 feet off the ground with nothing below.

But once she got the feel of the team effort, it was fun to feel the wind in her face and watch it billow her skirts past the fast-flying wheels.

"Hang on tight!" Michael called above the whistle of the wind.

When she hesitated, he called again, "Arms around my waist! The new pneumatic tires are guaranteed against blowout. Still, it's safer—"

Frightened, she grasped his waist with both hands and relaxed against him. His shoulders were broad in their tweed coat.

Safe. It was such a nice word. There should be safety in marriage . . . but Michael's kind or hers?

His family saw security in power—the kind that money and background afforded. But something vital was missing. Why, they were not a real family at all. More of a pack. That was it, a pack of animals—snarling, biting, fighting primitively underneath their polished finish—never ready to accept a new member until it was established who was leader!

Her own family found power only in love.

And, feeling as they and the other settlers did, they reached out with open arms to embrace the whole world. God was their Leader. . . .

"A penny for your thoughts!"

True jumped at Michael's words. She had been so absorbed in her thinking that she was unaware they had stopped.

"Where are we?" she murmured as Michael helped her dismount.

"Magnolia Manor, but we approached it from the other road. It's smoother."

True looked around her in dismay. Once this neglected ground had been a vast plantation—something she had not known. But now weeds and brambles had taken over. The ancient oaks, like bearded prophets, looked saddened by the change.

"Were the shacks ever occupied?"

"Still are—one of the many decisions you'll need to come to. Slaves' quarters and sharecroppers. Some of both still around. Guess they think they have squatters' rights now."

"I only saw where the big house stood—which reminds me, there's someone I want to ask about: Joshua, the gardener."

"They won't tell you here. Mostly, they act like scared rabbits—"

True silenced him with a finger to her lips. Her ears had picked up a faint moaning sound, followed by a mellow hum of voices which seemed to rise and fall in a melody that was a combination of poetry and music. The croon seemed a part of the setting.

Michael directed her gaze to the tumbledown shack, larger than the others, only a short distance away.

"Their church. These people spend more time on their knees than at the plow!"

"Maybe they know something we've not talked about," she said slowly. "Grandma Mollie, a wonderful friend of my family, used to say, 'Neither belly nor purse takes the place of God.' "

Michael sucked in his breath.

"And you believe that?"

"Of course I believe it!" True was unable to say more, as an unexpected need swept over her. "Michael, I want to go inside. Will you come with me?"

"In *there?*" Michael made no effort to hide his dismay. "Down here we don't mingle—by mutual agreement."

"I'm not sure it's mutual," True said. "And, after all, this is supposedly my property, so I don't have to have a welcoming committee. Back in Oregon we join together in caring for and nurturing one another . . . are you coming or not?"

Inside, the black worshipers, with heads bowed, continued the sad-sweet croon. The voices blended together in the sweetest music True had ever heard—music of the soul, born of suffering, yet triumphantly proclaiming that there was nothing—*nothing*—that God could not heal.

Entranced, True listened—how long she did not know. Maybe she would have stayed all day. But there was Michael to consider.

Reaching out to touch his hand, she signaled that they should go. Nobody had noticed their arrival. Nobody noticed their departure. Their spirits were in the "other world" of hope and faith.

"May I breathe now?" Michael grinned once they were outside. Then, more seriously, there in the shadow of the old building, he grasped her shoulders and gently turned her to face him.

"True, tell me something—just how important to you is all this?"

"These people—or my faith?"

"I have a strange feeling that you equate the two."

True nodded.

"The Bible gives us no choice . . . have you given any thought to it, Michael—love, in the context I mentioned?"

"Mostly I've wondered if it's a qualification for your husband."

True bit her lip in concentration. Then she spoke truthfully: "I don't know, Michael—I honestly don't know. Let's take it a step at a time about the husband . . . but as a father? I would have to say, yes, it's essential . . . that's the best

I can come up with right now. You see, I too am searching for answers—"

"And we won't find them here!" Michael's voice was lighter. "Can you walk in those shoes? Oh, yes, I see you can. Thank goodness you wore something sensible."

"I'm a pioneer woman, remember?" Her tone matched his. "Let's go!" And, picking up her skirts gingerly, she followed him as they hiked for what seemed miles over land which lay idle for lack, she suspected, of tools with which these deprived people could work.

Adults were either at the church or chose to remain out of sight in the buildings which leaned against giant oak trees for support. Several times True stopped to speak with the near-naked children, but they seemed so frightened that she gave up trying to visit with them.

When Michael asked if she had seen enough, True nodded. "But I would like to find out what happened to Joshua."

Michael shrugged.

"Drifted back to Shanty Town, most likely. Most of them are pretty shiftless."

True bit her lip.

"Don't spoil my day, Michael."

"Oh, darling, I didn't intend to. Forgive me. Please—let's make this our day. We are entitled to that."

Yes, they were. And with that, she took the hand he offered. Together they walked back to the spreading oak where Michael had left the bicycle. Gathering up the lunch basket, he smiled broadly.

"I really am a romantic soul. Look!"

True's eyes followed the direction that Michael's finger pointed. And there, chained to a gnarled cypress tree, was a canoe, complete with two paddles.

"I—I don't know," she began uncertainly. "I've never ridden in a boat. Our rivers are so swift—"

Michael laughed and, grabbing her arm, forced her forward.

"Fear not, Fair One! This is a shallow bayou."

The water, she found, was stale, stagnant, and murky. All the same, she stepped carefully into the canoe with a growing sense of adventure. With her offer to help, Michael tapped her nose lightly with an index finger.

"That's one of the things I like about you—your willingness to learn. But not until we're safely past this trap of water hyacinths. Just relax and let me tell you now the things I *love* about you."

"Not now, Michael. Please not now." True leaned back, allowing the sun to slope soothingly across her face only to disappear in the long drapes of Evangeline moss at frequent intervals.

Enjoy the sun and shade. Enjoy your companion. Time enough for talking, thinking, resolving later. . . .

Michael rowed on in silence. There seemed to

be no room for words—even those which must be spoken. Now and then he pointed out a rare bird haloed in shafts of sunlight against the patches of blue. There was no sound but for the unbroken song of the birds and the slap-slap of the oars against the water.

"Hungry?" Michael's question reminded True to note that the sun had passed high noon. "There's a clump of trees to the right with a little island in their midst." Without waiting for an answer, Michael turned the canoe toward it.

A few minutes later, True, leaning lazily against a rough-barked cypress, was engaging in Michael's game of trying to catch wild grapes he tossed at her mouth.

"Come now, is *this* all we carried in that hamper?" she laughed, missing a grape.

"I thought the belly wasn't important—" Michael began. Immediately, interrupting himself, he raised a conciliatory hand. "Strike that one and have a sugar-cured ham sandwich. Lucky for us Tisha saw to our needs. Cousin Emily would have suggested watercress—ouch! I beg your pardon again . . . she represents the 'purse,' doesn't she?"

In spite of herself, True laughed as she bit into a ham sandwich so reminiscent of Grandma Mollie Malone's that tears unexpectedly filled her eyes.

"I'm sorry," she whispered at the look of concern on Michael's face. "It's a day of sun and shadows—on the bayou and in my heart—and I can't ask you to understand. I don't even understand myself! I don't know who I am—"

In an instant Michael was by her side, having upset the lemonade in the middle of the tablecloth. Neither of them paid the slightest attention to the liquid's spread beneath the pile of sandwiches and toward the mint-jelly layer cake.

She was in his arms and they were clinging to one another. She should be pouring out her troubles. Telling him all about herself. There must be no secrets in love. But instead she had needed a shoulder to cry on. And Michael's was there.

The lunch went unfinished. Michael's lips brushed her cheeks again and again. They should be getting back. But a heavy languor held her still.

True let her half-closed eyes drink in the beauty of the afternoon sky, barely breathing, engulfed in warmth. And for a fleeting moment she was back in the glass bubble in which she was encased when she occupied Michael's luxurious suite en route from the Oregon Country to Atlanta, weightless, high above the earth.

Then she was brought back to earth.

"We must talk." This time it was Michael who said the words. "I have asked you to marry me. We can't keep putting the issue off."

"I know." True's voice was still dreamy, like that of a child who is not yet quite awake. "I know." Idly she tickled his ear with a blade of grass. "And I'm grateful."

"Grateful! Is that all you have to say to a proposal, True?" Michael's voice carried a faint edge of impatience.

"You deserve better, but there's so much we must clear up first . . . and there's something more," she added. Wide awake, True realized that she had to begin somewhere. Where better than with love itself?

"I have to consider what we talked about this morning—faith and all it involves. And, too, it seems to me that love has to grow slowly, steadily, based on—well, so many things."

Until, she thought, *two hearts beat as one.* . . .

Rising, Michael began to gather up the remains of the picnic. The dappled sunlight had turned gold with the promise of sunset. It was a beautiful time of day, but something had gone wrong—something she alone could correct.

Sadly, True stooped to fold the ends of the sodden linen tablecloth, wishing for her sake and his that she were ready to commit herself.

By the time they reached home the sun had set, leaving behind a rich burgundy glow to color the horizon behind the great house. As always, it looked silhouetted in mystery—some of which she must help clear. Screened away from the windows by heavy shrubs, True paused to look at Michael, trying to think of some word which would break the tension.

But caught in the transition between dusk and dark, Michael's face was closed—like that of a stranger—which, she realized, in many ways he was. With a sigh, she turned and walked toward the door, aware that the beautiful day had offered everything but what she had intended. She and Michael had not talked. And she had hurt him deeply.

• • •

Friday.
There was breakfasting with the family when the package arrived. When the butler announced that there with a parcel for "Missy No'th," she was aware of all eyes turned her direction.

Emily's were like burning coals and True was careful to avoid direct contact with them as she carefully folded her napkin, excused herself, and—with the small package in hand—hurried to the privacy of her room.

Wil, her heart sang out, *Wil, Wil, Wil!* She was expecting nothing from him, but whatever it was made no difference. It would put them in touch again.

Wil . . . Wil . . . it was like the heartbeat she had wanted to describe to Michael.

Clinging to the moment, True held the package to her pounding heart.

Savor the moment. Make it last. . . .

But when she saw the address her heart sank.

Her name, crudely printed, appeared to have been done by somebody who intentionally wished to disguise the handwriting. Unfamiliar, of course . . . and yet there was something about it . . . never mind!

She was weary from trying to solve unsolvable problems. Sick with disappointment, she tore the wrapping from a small box. Then, lifting the lid, she could only sink weakly into a chair, her mind unable to believe that the beautiful sapphire-and-pearl brooch lay there winking back at her.

What . . . who . . . well, she must find out. Quickly she picked up the wrappings and reexamined them in hope of finding a postmark. There was none.

"Now, Lord," she whispered, "you'll have to help me decide which ones to tell—"

At that moment there was a sharp rap on her door.

"True, there are two men downstairs wishing to speak with you!"

Emily! But why hadn't she sent one of the servants? Curiosity, of course, True realized angrily. Quickly, tucking the brooch away inside her bag and picking up all signs of the hastily opened package, she joined the older woman at the door without inviting her to come inside.

True followed Emily's straight-backed lead into the sunroom, where tuberous begonias, odorless in their confinement, separated great pots of Boston fern. One of the two men rose from an opulent chair. Stern-faced, he offered his hand.

"I am Edward Keith," he said, sweeping back thin, white hair with long fingers, "a private investigator whose services Mr. William St. John has engaged."

He turned to Emily, dismissing her with a look before introducing his companion. True was acutely aware of the rustle of angry skirts as Emily retreated.

Then she obediently sat down in one of the needlepoint-covered chairs, large enough for the three of them, to which the investigator pointed an inviting finger. Emily would be furious at being denied the privilege of being hostess.

"And this is Albert Berkshire, attorney-at-law." Wondering what the two men were doing here together, True found herself looking into a pair of merry eyes in a round, good-natured face, topped with a thatch of bright red hair. It was easy to answer his smile.

Edward Keith cleared his throat.

"Since Mr. St. John also wishes to have Attorney Berkshire draw up some legal documents, his business may take more time. If you will simply respond to my questions regarding the robbery first, then I shall be on my way. I am a very busy man."

"I'll be glad to cooperate, but it puzzles me why you are here—that is, were you aware that the adjusters have spoken with me?"

"My dear Miss North, that is precisely why I am here. There seems to be some irregularity—a matter," he paused significantly, "that you brought to the family's attention."

Michael had told his father, then. True wondered about Emily. And then she listened carefully to Edward Keith.

The investigation was brief. What else could she tell him about the man she had recognized? True described the man who had stood in the midst of the train robbers.

Seeming to agree, Edward Keith nodded, then asked her to get in touch with him immediately should Charles Devore make contact with her.

"Contact?" True frowned. "What would he want of me?"

"Never mind. I would not wish to frighten you—just do as I ask. If he suspects you recognized him, he might try to cover his tracks. Even pretend to recover the brooch. . . ."

The brooch! As if from a great distance True heard one of the two men ask if she was all right. Yes, but it was so warm.

A glass of water? Yes, that would be nice. Then she was shaking hands with the investigator, and Albert Berkshire was asking if she felt up to continuing.

Yes, she was fine now.

The lawyer shuffled through his briefcase, bringing out a fistful of papers.

"Now, nobody suspects you of being an impostor, Miss North. This is all routine. Strictly routine."

"I don't understand." Why had she said she was all right?

"My error. I took it for granted that you knew yourself to be an heir to Magnolia Manor. I will handle the details on the property for you. But it is not entirely because of the old plantation that I've come. It seems that Mr. St. John has evidence leading him to believe that you are entitled to railroad shares belonging jointly to the Kincaid-St. John-Kelly—er, Stein joint ownership but—" He paused, a frown creasing between his bewildered blue eyes.

"Is there a problem?" True found it hard to breathe.

"Well, yes, there does seem to be some kind of error made here." Then his merry face brightened. "Nothing you should worry your pretty head about, just confusion with names. I am sure you brought along identification."

"Identification?" The word was a whisper.

"Any statement by an attending physician would have sufficed." Albert Berkshire tapped on his teeth with his pen. "Oh," he said brightly, "a family Bible?"

"I never thought—I—the family Bible is in Oregon—"

He inhaled in concentration.

"Ordinarily, we could send for it. But in view of Mr. St. John's condition—tell me, can you give me the names of your four grandparents, including your grandmothers' maiden names? That would be a start. And your own father's full name—family lineage, you know?" He smiled.

Stunned, True could only stare at him.

"I have nothing at all," she said woodenly. "I only brought along maps, a little Bible, and my mother's diary to direct me—"

"Diary!" The ruddy face fairly glowed. "That is admissible!"

Admissible. And revealing. Tearing away every shred of privacy. Wordlessly, True handed him the diary.

• • •

Saturday.

There was a brief encounter with Michael early in the morning. Brief, and yet it took up, as if by plan, where the two of them had left off on the bayou. Michael was on his way upstairs to see his father. True was on her way downstairs to check on the morning mail. They met halfway and stood looking wordlessly at each other for a moment on the shadowy landing.

Then Michael spoke.

"I understand Father sent the investigator and attorney to see you. How did it go?" His question was made warm and personal by the reach of his hands to grasp and hold onto hers.

"Very well," she said without withdrawing her

hands. "I guess I wondered why they came together—"

"Expediency. Time is a factor. It's running
out."

"For us all," True murmured without meeting
Michael's gaze. "I want you to know that I'm
thinking—"

Help me say it, Michael. But he was silent. Her
question, when it came, was too abrupt.

But somewhere below there was the sound of
a door opening and closing, so hurriedly she
whispered, "Would you have been attracted to
me from the photograph? Your father told me—"

"He has told me everything—"

"About the circumstances of my birth?" she
gasped. "That too?"

"That too. Did you think it would make a
difference?"

"Yes. No. I don't know. I hadn't planned to
discuss it—certainly not with the others—"

Footsteps below. Michael spoke quickly.

"I think we're talking about different things."
His hands tightened and he drew her to him in
a quick embrace. "Nothing could alter my feelings—nothing." His voice was husky with emotion. "And to answer your question, which
somehow got lost in the conversation, yes, I
would have been attracted to you—and come to
love you just as my father loved your grandmother and your Aunt Mary Evangeline who
looked so like her!"

Her *aunt*. Michael didn't know. *Explain? But how?*

Now there were footsteps on the stair. The two of them drew apart, each going his separate direction. Even as Emily greeted True on the stairway (with unaccustomed warmth), her mind was on the secrets contained in her mother's diary.

They had been sacred to Angel Mother, then later to Aunt Chrissy, then to herself. Evidently, Albert Berkshire and William St. John intended to preserve its secrets, even from Michael.

Downstairs, True thumbed through the large stack of mail for the household. She had looked for mail from home for so long that she had all but given up hope of receiving any.

Home, and all those wonderful people who had been bigger than life so recently, now seemed to be receding into the past—diminishing in size as they faded into the beautiful background of her childhood. Maybe this was the real world . . . her past, the dream. . . .

But there were letters! Two from Aunt Chrissy and a bulky letter from Young Wil! She ran back up the stairs three at a time to be alone.

Lying across the great bed, forgetting to turn back the silk coverlet which just cleared the dust ruffles, True held his letter to her heart. It had begun the relentless tattoo again.

Young Wil . . . Young Wil . . . then wildly, *Wil, Wil, Wil!*

But dessert comes last, Grandma Malone had

taught her. Daddy had said it another way—that one did the toughest tasks first, then the others seemed easier. And from these teachings Young Wil had devised a game for her and Marty called "Anticipation." They *anticipated* how good a chocolate cake would be before testing a crumb. *Anticipated* the joys of opening gifts . . . and childhood habits are hard to break. Even if she wanted to!

So, happily anticipating the contents of her childhood idol's fat letter—all resentment dissolved like the morning fog along the bayou—True happily opened her aunt's letter bearing the earlier of the two postmarks.

Quickly she scanned it to make sure the whole family was well and safe. Later she would read it again and again. But for now, the heavy pounding of her heart forbade any deep thinking. Except anticipation!

Everyone was fine, Aunt Chrissy said. Fine and missing True . . . oh, how they missed her! Her being in Portland was different . . . within reach. . . . "But Atlanta—oh, darling, it's so distant in every way. Has it been kind to you?"

True raised her eyes to the high arch of the beamed ceiling, realizing for the first time what it must have cost Aunt Chrissy to leave home and family and make the long trek by stage alone.

Oregon was younger then, and more primitive. More dangerous, too. Prior to the Civil War, Atlanta must have possessed a beautiful culture, one which its colonial inhabitants fully planned would go on forever. What courage it must have taken to leave when Aunt Chrissy found herself jilted . . . jilted by the man she was to marry! And the reason still pained her . . . jilted because of True herself!

Which of the two half-sisters must have suffered the greater agony? she wondered. The one Jonathan Blake jilted or the youunger one whom he promised to marry for the sake of "decency."

Decency? True shuddered, wondering if thinking had changed here much today. The thought bothered her. She turned her full attention to her aunt's letter.

"You know how spectacular Oregon is now, wild apples ripening along the fencerows trying to outdo the orchards and the leaves on fire with color. The twins have staked claims on Halloween pumpkins, feeling sure Young Wil will be here to carve them the way he did for you and Marty? No, we don't hear. . . ."

Daddy Wil was keeping neighbors in good health . . . Miss Mollie was making green tomato pickles . . . the church had been able to find a new minister, recently retired and a fine man that Young Wil had worked with in Portland . . . in need of another teacher . . . the board was hoping True would return. . . .

The second letter was from the twins. The kittens were growing. They had a new dog, a shaggy one named "Beowolf." He was afraid of

154

cats, though. Would she be home for Halloween? Thanksgiving was too far away . . . and "On Christmas everybody has to be here. Young Wil will hang up six-foot stockings like always and Daddy will get a ten-times-bigger tree than ever!" That was Kearby.

"About Christmas," Jerome wrote, beginning where his sister left off, "we have to start early, so you'd better hurry home. We want the house real fancy—and there's a program at church. I'm a Wise Man who knows a lot. Kearby just sings in the angel chorus, but she'll do good. Daddy says she's got lusty lungs! Oh, True, come home. . . ."

And at the bottom, Daddy Wil had penned, "They're right, you know; Christmas began with a Child. It remains a time when each of us can be a child again—when we can celebrate our most precious possession, our family. A time for love!"

True had smiled through the children's letters. But at reading Daddy Wil's postscript, she wept.

Oh, darlings, her heart cried out, *don't you know how much I love you?* To which they would have asked, "Then what are you doing so far away?" And she would be unable to answer. But soon. Yes, soon now.

Anticipate. Anticipate! But, try as she would, waiting was impossible. True tore into Young Wil's letter, not caring that the tattered envelope fluttered all about the room.

My dear little True:

No broken bones since you left. Come to think on it, no bitten hands either! I still bear that scar. But no grudges. I have forgiven your transgressions since you went away. I simply never knew it was possible to miss anyone so much. . . .

True hugged the letter to her.

Oh, don't spoil it now, she whispered across the miles. *Don't tell me I am a "burden," "brat," "nuisance." I am a grown-up now. Remember how at Daddy Wil and Aunt Chrissy's wedding you said "Yes" to my proposal and promised we'd have an even bigger cake with three feet of white frosting?*

You really were a raw nerve "back when," but somehow you and I always understood each other. And I guess you were right. Even raw nerves heal in time! Meaning that your letter indeed sounded like my little-girl monster is growing up! Well, I've been waiting for that. . . .

Say it, say it! True's heart begged. *That I would make a suitable wife for a country doctor. A little of me's a teacher. A little bit's a nurse after my experience on the train. And ALL of me's head over heels in love with Young Wil North!*

Hungrily she read on. But the letter went on to other matters. They had always shared everything, so it made sense that he would continue the pattern.

His studies in pathology were drawing to a close. Following in the footsteps of Uncle Wil, his research of the common cold was up for review for possible publication. He was doing an internship in "bedside manners," and, of course, he continued the botany collections. Church work took up a lot of time, so it was good that he had found a young lady at the rooming house who could help him "the way you did with my notes."

True's heart sank. Someone had replaced her? Why, Young Wil had said nobody, absolutely nobody, else could read his writing—and his mind.

Halfheartedly she read on. But the rest of the letter was mostly in response to her account of the long trip . . . expressing the proper amount of concern over her having been a victim of the robbery and showing thankfulness for her safety—but also having the good sense not to imply an "I told you so!"

Of course he wouldn't do that. He was never accusing, just protective. Overly so, she used to fume. Now she longed for his care . . . but why was it necessary to find another girl? Weren't there boys who could assist?

Yes, there was Marty, if he would stick around long enough.

She reread the sentence, anger rising a little. After all, did he have to say *young?* She had avoided the adjective when describing Michael.

157

Well, not anymore! She would begin a letter right away, and her words, she hoped, would be as biting as her teeth once had been! How could he understand her and be so blind?

True was to read his letter until it was frayed about the edges and the writing smudged with tears, reading into it something new each time, like the game they had played as children, chanting "He loves me," "He loves me not" as they plucked petals from the daisy fields in the summer sun.

Always her daisy promised "He loves me." But, admittedly, she had cheated a little sometimes. Maybe she was doing the same with the letter, making the first part read "He loves me" and allowing mention of this girl who had usurped her place to deny Young Wil's love.

But for now she must not sit "mooning around" (Grandma Mollie's expression). There was a quick letter to Young Wil to write, another to Aunt Chrissy.

And then she must find Emily Kincaid and explain that she would be going to Boston, and then perhaps back to Oregon, as soon as business here was finished.

Something else bothered her, a little feeling of something she had left unsaid. Oh, yes, she should explain that her reason for staying on at this house for the brief time remaining was because of William St. John's request. Emily would be displeased.

But she wasn't. To True's dismay, the woman was cordial.

"Well, I should hope you would be staying! Haven't we appeared hospitable?"

"Well, yes—" True, off guard, realized she sounded tentative. But Emily, like everything about this place, confused her.

"As a matter of fact, I have planned a party for you next Saturday evening. It will take the servants that long to prepare properly. And I suppose you will wish to do some shopping?"

Buy yourself a new gown. Don't embarrass us.

True inhaled deeply. A party in her honor. Without a "by-your-leave." How was she being presented? As a *shareholder?* Surely not "family." Not until she and Michael talked again.

What would this arrogant woman say if she refused to attend? True was on the verge of speaking when Emily, having settled the matter in her own mind, glanced at the tiny jeweled watch pinned to her blouse and said, "Oh, I was to tell you that Cousin William wishes to see you in his quarters. I wouldn't stay long—"

Woodenly, True rose. Why wasn't she able to say no to these people? Obviously she didn't belong here. Emily had made it clear from the beginning—until now. There was a sudden . . . what was it? *Softening?* No, more like a resignation.

"By the way, dear," Emily called to True's departing back, "I'm so glad Michael found you!" True stiffened and waited, knowing what would come next. "We needed to locate the missing shareholder and set matters straight. No longer a need to fence!"

And then be off with you? Who knew what this woman was thinking? True realized anew as she hurried up the stairs that she was unaccustomed to such complicated people.

Family and friends in the Oregon Country nurtured one another. "Fencing" to them meant patching up the zigzagging rails—not holding one another at sword's point!

William St. John looked even more fragile than when True had seen him before. It was hard to tell if he was breathing except for the small rise and fall of the brocade coverlet.

In the shadows she moved toward him, like one of the shadows herself. But he saw her, motioned her closer, and motioned a white-uniformed nurse to bring something from one of the large wardrobes which lined the east wall of the bedroom.

True gasped with delight when the woman wordlessly held up a dress for her inspection. Of exquisite silver net, the gown was trimmed below the sweetheart neckline with all-over silk-lace medallions. Minute white satin bows rippled in row after row around the blouse, stopping at a wide, crushed-velvet belt of palest blue at the waist. There insertion of valencinnes lace raced in vertical symmetry up and down the floor-length sweep of the wide skirt. And underneath

160

there seemed to be a dozen daintily ruffled silk petticoats—pale blue to match the belt.

"How beautiful!" True whispered when she could breathe. "A wedding gown?" She moved to touch the garment. The fabric seemed to take on life when her fingers touched the sleeping folds.

"Hers . . . for our almost-wedding. . . ." The voice was faint.

Hers? That would mean Grandmother's dress! True touched it again, almost reverently.

"Yours now . . . wear it to the party . . . just for me. . . ."

True gave a little cry and ran to kneel beside the man who might have been her grandfather. "Oh, I would be so honored!"

William St. John stirred slightly and turned his head so he could meet her eyes.

"I saved her trunk . . . from fire . . . no other wedding dress . . . two husbands . . . but loved me!"

The last three words came out triumphantly in spite of the beads of perspiration spelling exhaustion on the pale forehead. The nurse motioned her to go—when there was so much to say.

Gently, True kissed the old man's cheek and left the room.

161

17

Unfinished Business

There was more unfinished business here than True had thought when she spoke to Emily about leaving. Before going to Boston, she wished to visit the cemetery where her grandparents lay and, if possible, to locate the grave of her mother's first husband.

Aunt Chrissy had wanted her to do that and had drawn a map so complete that she would need no help. That was good, for True wished to make the journey alone. Only in that way could her ancestors "come alive" completely, though already she was seeing them in a new light—the too-fragile spirit of her grandmother and the clay of her grandfather.

Their common blood flowed through her own blood. And yet, True realized, they were as foreign to her as the occupants of the strange mansion.

There was a Sunday-feel to the air the morning True set out alone to visit her grandparents' graves. Church bells tolled an invitation all over the city, but after the depressing experience at the old church in which her mother and aunt had been forced to "worship" in a kind of piety they could never understand, she felt no desire to respond.

She would have preferred going to the falling-down building on the premises of Magnolia Manor.

"I could identify with them—I know I could," True had insisted to Michael.

But he had said (perhaps wisely), "Yes, but could they identify with you?" Probably not—not now, anyway.

So today I will worship God in my own way, she decided as she dressed the minute the family carriage was out of sight. Taking her Bible, she hurried along the cobblestone streets toward the ruins of her mother and aunt's childhood home.

Getting away alone had been difficult: first pleading a slight headache to appease Emily, then convincing Michael, who refused to attend services without her, that she needed a walk to clear her head. No company. *Alone.*

Pausing at a sun-dappled corner to get her bearings, True fanned herself with the folded map before opening it to see if she were nearing the site.

No breeze swayed the moss, and the hot sun drew up unpleasant odors from the stagnant bayou. Mosquitoes buzzed about her head, and somewhere among the bullrushes a bullfrog complained hoarsely. Otherwise it was quiet. Too quiet. So still that True could hear her own breathing on the heavy air.

Feeling alone and uneasy, she checked the map quickly.

"Here it is!" She said the words aloud, for to her surprise the cemetery joined the far corner of Magnolia Manor—just a stone's toss from the building where the ex-slaves and sharecroppers worshiped together. Somehow the discovery pleased her.

The cemetery was all but hidden by a dense forest of bearded oaks. Once inside the gate, which seemed to hover jealously over the churchyard, True stood and looked around in dismay.

From the outside it had appeared overgrown with blackberry vines. But inside all the brambles were cleared away from the gravesites. True wondered who was responsible. She had to pick her way slowly through the mounds as there were soft bogs and oozing pools, some of which looked treacherous if she should stumble and fall.

It was hard to see in the deep shade of the hanging moss. Here and there tombstones showed dim white in the darkness. Crudely constructed wooden crosses marked some of the graves. The other mounds, appearing more recent, were unmarked.

Nervously she made her way from one headstone to another, reading names and dates in the yellow twilight of the moss's shade. The old church stood some distance away, but there was no sign of life.

Remembering the warning from Investigator

Edward Keith that her life might be in danger until Charles Devore was apprehended, a shudder passed through her body. The idea was no longer as ridiculous as before.

With a pounding heart she moved on unsuccessfully until suddenly a tall, white monument—largest and most elaborate of them all—loomed ahead. Even before she could reach the site, slipping and sliding from time to time, she knew it would be the place of her grandparents' interment.

Lifting her skirts above the oozing earth, she leaned down and found their names, rechecked Aunt Chrissy's notes, and found that the dates matched.

There were no children belonging to the Stein family except her mother, who was buried back in Oregon beside Uncle Joe.

Why then should there be three graves here with a common gravestone? Curiously, she moved slightly in order to read the lettering, only to feel her head reel with surprise. KELLY!

Why, that would be Aunt Chrissy's father . . . why wouldn't her aunt have known? And what were the remains doing here when the map showed the grave in a secluded southeast corner? It had been a long time, but her aunt was one to remember details.

This was something she would want to share, but for the moment True felt a need to search out her own feelings . . . to meditate . . . and somehow identify with a past she could never share in order to understand herself and her strange feelings of being torn between the two worlds in which her mother had lived.

Quietly she knelt at the foot of the center grave. This was her grandmother, with a husband lying on either side. And yet True was disappointed that she felt nothing but curiosity concerning the woman like whom her own mother and she herself looked.

Something, however, compelled her to remain, to open her Bible, and read some of her favorite passages: "The Lord is my Shepherd: I shall not want. . . ."; "In my Father's house are many mansions. . . ."; "Lo, I am with you always. . . ." Then, closing her eyes, she prayed for a long, long time.

When a twig snapped behind her, True jumped. Fully expecting to see Charles Devore, it came as a great surprise to see the face of Michael instead. But his words were an even greater surprise.

"Which of the two men was your grandfather, True?"

His voice was low and expressionless. True answered in the same tone. "Does it make a difference?"

"In the will, yes. Even though the money and property came from the Kelly family, it went to the Stein chap—due to, I would say, a lack of business acumen on your grandmother's part."

"But to you—would it make a difference to you?"

Michael's answer was to reach down, pull her to her feet, and brush the caking mud from her skirt.

"Look at you. You're a mess!" Lightly. As if the previous conversation had never been.

That was one of the things that infuriated her about this man. One second he was cold, aloof, probing shrewdly. The next he was warm, charming, and often teasing. He was a puzzle, like everything and everybody else here. Well, what had she expected of him anyway?

Being a Stein entitled her to money, a source of power. But it admitted illegitimacy . . . how had Emily phrased it? "Bastardy child!" Well, there was no power in a "bastardy wife"! His hesitation had answered adequately.

True jutted out her chin and was about to say she had an answer for him when something in the shadows stopped her. Just a slight movement. It could have been the wind, except that there was no breeze. Wordlessly, she pointed a shaking finger toward what appeared to be the figure of a man squatting behind one of the gravestones. Michael's eyes followed her finger.

"A man," she whispered. "He's gone now—but there was one—"

"Let's get out here!" Michael grasped her arm and hurried her from the churchyard.

18

Fast-Moving Events

"We must give all our attention to the party this week," Emily said as she and True shared an early breakfast.

True had risen before the sun, hoping for time to write to Aunt Chrissy, give her a report, and make sure everything was all right. Something about her aunt's last letter had bothered her. It was nothing she could put her finger on—just one of Miss Mollie's "feelin's" that something was amiss.

Was it Marty's long absences—or could she be right in suspecting that Young Wil was involved with the girl he had spoken of and her aunt did not want her to be hurt?

One minute she was telling herself that it made no difference. But in the next one, she knew better. Any woman who tried to take her place . . .

"True!" Emily, who had interrupted her plans, now interrupted her thoughts.

"We'll open the entire downstairs into a ballroom . . . chamber music . . . banks of flowers there. . . ."

True only half-heard. Ballroom? Emily was giving a *ball*? And in her honor? It made no sense. She had thought of only a few selected friends. But this was too much!

"You have given thought to the proper gown? I can help you choose what is correct."

"I have the proper gown," True said softly, taking pleasure in the look of perplexity that crossed Emily's face. "I—"

But whatever else she felt must be said had to wait. Hosea appeared at the door to announce that there was a gentleman to see Miss North. Would Missy True join him in the library?

Edward Keith rose from one of the ladder-back chairs when True entered the room.

"I wanted you to know, Miss North," the investigator said without preliminaries, "that two of the men you helped identify as bandits are in custody. One, however, remains at large—as does Charles Devore. May I remind you how important it is that you stay in touch with us? If either should make contact in any way or you see anything suspicious—?" Inspector Keith ran a hand through his white hair, pale eyes questioning like his tone of voice.

True was tempted to tell of the mysterious return of the brooch. But something made her ask instead, "Which of the men did the authorities take into custody?"

The man looked at her, his eyes boring into hers.

"You would recognize names?" When she shook her head, feeling foolish that she had asked, he went on, "I can only say then that it was the tall one with the scar and the other one you described as medium-height. The third—have you remembered what you saw that seemed familiar?"

That his eyes were familiar, True wanted to say. But the words would not come. It was her duty to cooperate. To tell of the brooch and help identify the man if she could . . . but the moment was gone. The inspector, hat in hand, was giving her another warning to be cautious.

"Your life could depend on it!"

"Wait!" As if suddenly awakened from slumber, True's words tumbled over one another. "There was something strange—a man in the cemetery. I know I saw him dodge behind a marker."

Inspector Keith scribbled a note on his pad. "Alone?"

"He was. I wasn't. Michael was with me. But he didn't see the man and rushed me away. He seemed alarmed, but he has nothing to fear from this man—and I doubt if I do either."

"Let me be the judge of that!" His words were sharp. "As to the younger Mr. St. John—no, nothing to fear from Devore. His hasty departure was most likely to avoid trouble with the—uh, people who live on the property."

"The colored people?"

"And poor white trash."

True felt her back stiffen, and the pulse at the base of her throat begin to throb.

"I will never understand you people—never in a million years," she said in a voice that was carefully low and controlled. "You speak of the poorly educated and culturally deprived people as if they were less than your horses! How can they be other than they are when they're so ill-used—kept living in a world of unrelieved grimness?"

Unaware that her eyes were purple with rage, True turned her burning gaze on Edward Keith and was pleased to see that he was unable to return her gaze.

"I would be careful down here, Miss North," he said as if determined to make a point. "Even when they've done you a favor—"

"Go on!"

"Well, like moving the remains of your grandmother's first husband—pretty poor taste, if you ask me."

"I didn't ask!" True's words came out sharper than she intended because of the emotions stirring inside her. So the pitiful poor who inhabited the land she was about to own were responsible for seeing that their loved ones were together. The idea had such strong appeal that she spoke her thought aloud.

"Jesus would have loved these people."

True hardly heard the man leave. Two plans had taken shape in her mind. One she would discuss with the good-natured lawyer, who reminded her so much of Grandma Malone's Irish husband, O'Higgin, back home. The other she would manage herself. On the night of the great ball!

* * *

"You're quite sure, miss, that this is what you want to do, now are you?" Albert Berkshire's red eyebrows that matched his flaming hair rose in astonished arcs above his blue eyes. "Really, you're a remarkable young lady!"

True smiled at the attorney.

"Thank you for the compliment, Mr. Berkshire. And, yes, I'm quite sure what I want to do with the land if you're sure I own it."

"Mr. St. John, Sr., and I have gone over every word!"

"Does Michael know?"

Albert Berkshire stroked his forehead with a pudgy finger.

"No, nobody besides Mr. St. John, you and me. And I'm not sure anybody else should be informed—not yet."

True answered quickly.

"Oh, I agree! But you *do* think we can count on the government to help—I mean, offer a means of protection against protests?"

"Oh, they'll cooperate all right—even if it means sending in a militia! The government gave

172

a land grant some time ago as a possible site for the school adjacent to Magnolia Manor. Major Radfield was pleased when I located the legal owner of the property and is drafting a letter of appreciation to you. As to the new church, how much of the planning will you leave to the—"

"New owners?"

The attorney smiled broadly.

"Sure enough!" He smiled. "They won't be 'squatters' anymore!" He turned to look at her thoughtfully. "Are you sure you wish to break the news this way? I mean, if you change your mind—"

"I won't change my mind! This has been one of the reasons Emily didn't like me, hasn't it, Mr. Berkshire? She wanted the colored people and the poor whites out—am I right?"

Mr. Berkshire scratched his head.

"That she did, but to say she didn't *like* you—well, now, let's not be jumping to conclusions. Young Michael has some say—there now, I'm out of line, having made you blush. Back to business—you want what funds as are left after settlement costs to go into the building fund which I'm to hold in trust?"

"Right," True said, feeling a thrill of sheer joy race up and down her spine. "Let the new owners do their own planning . . . advising only as you need to. It may take some time for them to grow accustomed to making choices. . . ."

Mr. Berkshire blew his nose, reminding True again of O'Higgin.

"You know, Miss North, you've a great big heart."

True smiled mistily.

"Big hearts run in my family," she smiled. "And speaking of families, you have drawn up the proper papers regarding the railroad stock?"

"Sure enough! Half in your name, hereinafter known as the 'party of the first part'—meaning Stein—and the remainder in your aun't name, Christen Elizabeth Kelly Craig Wilson." He smiled, then continued, " 'party of the second part'—meaning Kelly, splitting dividends . . . reimbursing Oregon investors."

"Affirmative!" True smiled. And then they burst into shared laughter. First at the legal jargon, then for the sheer joy of having conspired to do something daring which would bring more happiness to the impoverished people of Magnolia Manor and back home than they ever knew existed.

With all the problems that faced her, True had never felt as happy and fulfilled in her entire life. She knew now that she had been right in coming here. She also knew where she belonged.

"I can't thank you enough, Mr. Berkshire. Now, when I finish in Boston . . . tell me, do you think it is safe for me to go?"

"Alone? Negative! I shall accompany you, of course."

19

The Daughter You Never Knew!

Displeasure colored Michael's face and his disposition when True announced that she would be going to Boston the following day. Why hadn't she told him? Well, they had had little time together, True tried to explain. But inside she was thinking that even those short times were tense. There were silences . . . spaces . . . unvoiced questions . . . and something akin to suspicion. There was everything to say. Or was there nothing?

"I thought you understood you were not to go alone," Michael said darkly, his voice in tune with a low rumble of thunder.

"Mr. Berkshire will accompany me. I need his advice." *Not yours.* True had not intended the implication. But it was there.

"I see." It was hard to tell if the tone said he was angry, annoyed, or hurt. Whatever they had shared had never been solid, and now words left unspoken were undermining any hope of permanence. True found herself thinking that although in every way he was the more sophisticated, it was she who saw farther. She could stare from the window of her heart and see something his eyes were unable to discern. Another world. Another way of life. Compassion. Love. *Family*—real family, born of trials, tears, and togetherness. And the even-larger family of God. . . .

As if reading her thoughts, Michael said almost angrily, "It's your religion, isn't it?"

Nate Goldsmith, chairman of the board of trustees back in the settlement, used to advise, "Ain't fittin' t'answer in anger, best run through th' books of the Old Testament." Only there wasn't time, so True inhaled deeply instead.

"I prefer the word *faith*, Michael. But, by either name, what could my beliefs have to do with the trip to Boston?"

"And you can deny that something has come between us?" The words were scornful.

"We have settled nothing," she said slowly. "Or have we?"

"That, my dear, was to have been *my* question . . . well, you run along to Boston on your secret mission—"

"There's nothing secret about it! I told you all along—"

"You've told me nothing really!"

We're quarreling. Actually quarreling. And I'm not sure what it's all about. Maybe they had better get everything out in the open. But when True turned to face him, the sound of Mr. Berkshire's voice reminded her that he was waiting.

"Michael—" she began. But he spun on his heel and was gone.

176

There was rain all the way to Boston. The train trip could have been lonely and frightening without the company of the red-haired attorney. Away from the environment of the Atlanta mansion, he became almost boisterous—laughing, reminiscing about his Canadian boyhood, and even singing some of his native songs. He was easy to talk to, and True found herself sharing a great deal that she had felt would be of little interest to the Kincaids and St. Johns. They talked of the forests, the streams, the mountains, and their mutual love for the kinds of people who had given their all to conquer the frontier and be conquered by it.

"Can you be happy away from the wild beauty of the Oregon Country, really happy?" Mr. Berkshire asked suddenly. His question did not seem out of order.

"I don't know," True said honestly. "I've wondered."

"You haven't said yes to the young man, then?"

"True smiled. "Neither have I said no." Then, before she knew the words would be coming, she mused aloud, "I'm not sure—not as sure as I think a girl should be . . . and I have a strange feeling that Michael isn't either."

Mr. Berkshire's merry eyes suddenly sobered. "Now what would make you think that? He proposed. He told me so!"

"But that was before—before he knew that I

was conceived out of wedlock . . . and that I have chosen to give most of my inheritance away. . . ."

Albert Berkshire sighed. "I am only an attorney who deals in facts—not at all skilled in matters of the heart. But, you know," he cocked his round head to one side, "I would say that if those things make a difference, you are indeed wise in postponing a decision!"

True was silent, weighing his words.

"Will you teach if you remain here?" There is a need for governesses—"

"Nothing like that!" she assured him. "What I would enjoy is impossible. If I could help out in the school that's coming one day to Magnolia Manor . . . or even go in as a nurse there. . . ."

She told him then about Aunt Chrissy's teaching, her mother's nursing, and her love for both. "I'm prepared in both fields—but mostly I guess I'm more prepared to be a wife and mother."

"And I beg you to wait for just the right man!"

"I know who the right man is—it's only—"

The train lurched at that point. And shortly afterward the conductor was singing out, "Boston, capital and largest city of the Commonwealth of Massachusetts, latitude 42 degrees and 21 minutes north. . . ."

His long, well-rehearsed orientation for passengers was still in progress when Albert Berkshire and True North stepped out and walked on. Visit the old cemeteries, monuments, and memorial tablets . . . like the King's Chapel Bury Ground and the Granary, where Boston's earliest celebrities lay resting.

But there was no time for this, of course. True looked around her at the busy, bustling city and wished with all her heart that she could tour it all. There was so much history here, so much she would want to share with the family, particularly Young Wil, who shared her interest in the Puritan values and their influence on the New World. It would soon be Thanksgiving, a good time. . . .

But the map that Aunt Chrissy drew (all guesswork, she admitted) did not fix the churchyard as being near the points of interest. "It looks closer to the sea," she said, pointing to the "X" her aunt had made. Mr. Berkshire agreed.

The cemetery was easier to find than True expected. So was the grave of Jonathan Blake. A caretaker pointed out a grassy knoll surrounded by a wrought iron fence as the Blake family's burial ground. "Fine old family. All gone now. You're the first visitor I recollect," the white-haired man volunteered. "Relative?"

True squared her shoulders. "His daughter," she said.

Albert Berkshire tactfully remained outside the enclosure. True stood silently at the foot of her father's grave, trying to picture the once-boyish, carefree manner . . . his devil-may-care attitude toward life . . . his ability to ruin the lives of the two women she loved. But the vision would not come. She felt only sadness that sometimes that's the way life was.

And in that moment she forgave her father.

"A new headstone you'll have—which says *IN MEMORY-from the daughter you never knew.*"

20

Brief Encounters

With the elaborate reception so near at hand, True tried to feel happy. Let anticipation take over. After all, wasn't this what every girl dreamed of? Something right out of a novel? But such reasoning brought no happiness. Instead, she felt vaguely uneasy and depressed. A certain air of expectancy hung over the great mansion. But it seemed born of frenzy. People hurrying, checking lists, speaking curtly. Undoubtedly, everything was perfectly executed. Exactly on schedule. Time for everything—except each other.

True had her share of rushing to do, too. Tisha, who thrived on secrets she had found, located a dressmaker who could nip the waist of her grandmother's gown a wee bit. And the seamstress, a nonstop talker, knew just the right hairdresser.

"Why, I've never had my hair done!" True had tried to object.

And the dressmaker replied, "But you've never been to a ball, you tell me—and certainly any young lady who's the honoree—"

So why not concede? Make it a dream come

true. But True wished with all her heart that she could generate enthusiasm, feel the way she felt the night Young Wil took her to the first square dance, following the roof-raising of the new school. She had missed every call . . . been late getting back to every corner . . . hearing and seeing nothing but her partner's face as he sashayed back and forth, meeting her eyes, making her feel alive, grown-up, and head-over-heels in love. How odd that a memory could start her blood circulating faster, while present anticipation only slowed its flow. . . .

The memory refused to go away, but True forced herself to work around it. She paid a quick call to Mr. St. John, giving him a briefing on what had been accomplished and what remained to be done. It hurt her to see that he was failing, but the hurt was eased by his tight grip on her hands even with his eyelids closed to all but words. It was as if he clung to her for life—life she felt would end soon after his present mission was done.

"I will come to you for final inspection before the ball," True promised, to which he said, "God bless you, Granddaughter!"

Granddaughter! That might have been. But, had circumstances gone another direction, perhaps she could have been the granddaughter of Emily Kincaid. The thought wiped away her smile. Like Grandma Mollie Malone said, "Best leave them things to the Lord. He knows a heap more'n the storks He created!"

Emily seemd to be everywhere at once. "Only the *grande monde* will be appearing. Make sure you reserve time for your personal appearance—if you're through poking around in graveyards. . . ." When her voice trailed off, True assured her that she had found what she needed, keeping her voice as civil as possible.

Emily allowed a list she was checking to flutter to the floor. "You found that they—those *terrible* people have exhumed my Jimmy's body—moved it by *her*—" True held back any words she might have spoken. For in that one revealing moment Emily had shown her vulnerability. What a lonely, barren life of hatred and distrust she had built for herself! What a prison for her tortured soul, on which everyone she met must help pay the taxes! "Yes, I saw," True said, her voice appropriately sad. But the sadness was for Emily. . . .

The days sped by. A letter came from Aunt Chrissy saying Young Wil had heard from Marty. Nothing more. True took a small margin of one afternoon to respond, giving a summary of her findings here. Then she mailed another novella-length letter to Young Wil, mentioning Michael liberally, but closing with "Love." The day before the party there was another bulky letter from him. Reluctantly True tucked it away for reading later, as Mr. Berkshire had some papers needing her signature and a report to make.

On the way to the conservatory where he waited, she had a brief encounter with Michael. His eyes looked restless and hungry—as if to say he had missed her. But they did not touch. His hand made a small movement toward her, then fell to his side, as if he felt there should be some more on her part.

Don't ask me now . . . I'm not ready! Her heart cried out, even as she wondered why he waited. His voice, when he spoke, was strained. "You seem different somehow," he said. He seemed less certain of himself.

"We all change," she murmured. "But I still don't know who I am . . . and I can't plan a future until I know *which* past I am!"

21

Love Leads Home

True found Young Wil's letter infuriating, frightening, and heartbreakingly beautiful. *What a hybrid you are, Wil North!* She laughed and cried at the same time. And then she lay silent and pensive, eyes violet in concentration as she gazed at the ceiling of her bedroom on Saturday morning. There were a million details needing her attention—none as important as the wonderful man who could do battle with words or tame the wild creatures of the forest. Nobody, *nobody*, she lay thinking, could string words together—like his thoughts—in a strange necklace of subordinate clauses and make them come out making sense. Nobody but Young Wil North, the one who claimed logically that he had loved her before she was born!

Why, then, did he choose to break her heart? And always in grandstand-play style!

It was infuriating and downright humiliating to have him speak so boldly of "this young lady." His too-casual references (too frequent, too!) were an open taunt. He might as well have quoted their Grandma Malone who dished out such phrases. Their surrogate grandmother loved saying, "When the cat's away, the mice're bound t'play!" just to make Irish O'Higgin's face turn redder.

"Me Mollie girl's causin' me heart t'miss!" he would say, plunging a fork into another of his wife's sourdough biscuits. "Well, yer hand shure ain't!" And, with that, she would swat the big, capable hand for its transgression against good manners. *Goodness! How I would like to see them. . . .*

True dried her eyes and forced her mind back to Young Wil's insults. Miss Mollie and O'Higgin were funny. Young Wil was not!

The letter repeated a list of "this young lady's" fine qualities—even made mention that Marty found her most appealing. Marty! Aunt Chrissy had said Young Wil was in touch. Why, then, didn't he tell her more? And why on this green earth was he introducing "this young lady" to their adopted brother? It would be like him to take her to meet the rest of the family. Which is exactly what he told her in the next paragraph he might do.

Oh, the nerve of him! If he were here to see her, she would tear this letter to shreds and say, "There! So much for your skirt-chasing, Portland ways!" But, without him as an audience, what was the use? And, besides, something else caught her eye.

"Glad about the railroad shares! Doesn't that make you a grand duchess or something? At any rate, the ownership will ease some tension on our brother's part, wouldn't you say? He never did, as our self-appointed 'Grandmam' says, 'cotton' to the right-of-ways they claimed through the farm grounds. . . ."

True read on, hoping he would say more about Marty. Instead, he expressed concern over what he called "Chrissy's anxiety." The two of them had always been close, True recalled. Aunt Chrissy had favored Young Wil when, orphaned, he came to live with the man she was later to marry—favored him and loved him above all the other children in her class. Partly, True suspected, because the little boy understood rejection, just as Aunt Chrissy did. She frowned.

If Young Wil had noticed, it wasn't only her own imagination that something was wrong at home. That was the thought that frightened her about the letter. Maybe Aunt Chrissy needed her . . . certainly not "this girl"!

But, infuriated and frightened as she was, True could only clasp the letter to her heart in sheer joy when in it Young Wil became the man she had toddled after in her babyhood, worshiped in her adolescence, fought with in her stormy teens—and now loved in the way that comes only once in a lifetime. A soulmate, helpmate—a man she could never do without! How could she ever have thought she could get along without him?

It's unfortunate that I can't paint words—use tinted ones or set them in slow motion . . . or write them in music, so you can see them rustling between the lines and spaces, ready for synchronizing into dream-flutes and dream-drums (including some re-membered half-notes of your frowning, fuming, and raging!) . . . or perhaps add the fragrances they deserve. Yes, unfortun-ate, that words, as Paul wrote, are "become as sounding brass or a tinkling cymbal," depreciating their value when I would so like to describe my feeling about the sights, sounds, and *feelings* we have shared. The beauty was there Halloween, but I didn't see it. The beauty will be there Thanksgiv-ing, but I will not taste it. But Christmas? There is so much we must say, so I take heart from Uncle Joe's last sermon. Remem-ber? "Love leads home," he said. . . .

22

Cinderella's Ball

Every crystal prism on the age-old chandeliers was dusted to shine like new moons. Every potted rubber plant, glistening from a coat of oil, reflected the rainbow colors. Chair rails glowed with rubbed-down wax. All doors leading to the verandas were swung open to admit a balmy breeze and give a view of the gardens beyond. Marble floors, stripped free of furniture except for chairs lined against the walls of three-rooms-made-into-one for the evening, waited for the whirl of dancing feet. The voices of those occupying the chairs were pitched low with expectancy. The chamber music was soft and sweet. . . .

And now there is a hush, a pause in the music, and the golden princess at the top of the stairs begins to descend. The stairs are long and winding—wide enough for an escort, but she is alone as she seems to float down. She is beautiful, so beautiful—her lemon-colored hair piled high, held in place by a little bouquet of violets placed there by her grandfather. The guests twitter, wondering if the owner of this mansion did not indulge in some youthful indiscretion. At the landing, the beautiful princess pauses, allowing the reflected light from the stained-glass window to tangle in her hair—turning it from pale silver to purest gold. Then, looking quickly over her shoulder as if for some sweet prince, she gathers her voluminous blue-and-silver skirts and, with a faint smile on her cameo-face, moves down the vast expanse of steps.

Who is she? What is this all about?

True can feel their questions. The frowning, fuming of them. The raging, racketing, rioting—and, for some, weeping in the words unsaid. How right Young Wil was! Words could never "phosphoresce." Words would not tell that she, an outward Cinderella, was unchanged inwardly. Just weeks earlier this same girl was in what they would have termed "rags." Admittedly, when she and Young Wil ran wildly over the meadows looking for a first daisy, her hair had hung down to her shoulders. All this was before these "fairy godpeople" undertook to transform her . . . away from her world—not of sweeping ashes from the hearth necessarily, but living an uncomplicated life among all kinds of people who exchanged recipes, waited on the sick, and knew little of each other's background and less about railroad shares and mansions. . . .

The Cinderella story had staked a claim on True's heart when Angel Mother and Daddy Wil told tales before the wood-gobbling fireplace in what the family called the "Big House." Later, in her little-girl grief over the loss of her mother, Young Wil repeated it over and over . . . and she cried . . . cried for her mother . . . cried for Cinderella, who, at the stroke of midnight, went back to her cinders . . . and cried for a whole world of sadness she was unable to understand. But now here it was again. The Cinderella story. As powerful as always. And beckoning, beckoning. Promising that she could inherit the world. If she would but sacrifice her soul. . . .

True closed her eyes for a brief moment to clear her head. Then, lifting her chin as one would expect of royalty, she let her eyes travel about the room in search of Prince Charming. At first she did not see Michael. Instead, her eyes met those of Emily Kincaid. Emily's eyes held a strange mixture of pride and hostility—part fairy godmother, part wicked stepmother. No matter what her identity, the other woman looked stunning in a forest-green velvet gown, trimmed richly with ecru lace.

When their eyes met, Emily said something to the distinguished-looking man at her side and came forward. She greeted True with such a warm embrace that anyone would doubt there existed any tension. True felt a rush of gratitude. Emily was trying to make the evening perfect, letting True be the center of this strange stage—the embrace serving to remind the guests, of course, that it was Emily herself who placed her there.

"How lovely you look, my dear," Emily said,

her voice inaudible to all ears but True's in the spattering of polite applause. "How elegant the sapphire-and-pearl brooch would have been—"

Strange that she would think of the brooch, a piece of jewelry she had never seen and certainly did not know had been returned. True had wanted to wear it, but something warned her to keep it in her bag. The warning of Investigator Keith? No, something more—the eyes of the one member of the trio she had been unable to identify. Because she knew now that whoever owned those eyes had recognized her, too. It was he who returned the brooch.

With her thoughts so far afield, True had missed her cue. Somehow she was being handed over to Michael. And together they stepped back into the pages of the Cinderella story. She, adorned and beautiful (her only dowry), exchanging offerings with a Prince Charming who could lay material things at the toes of her glass slippers. But he had no spiritual offerings.

Michael extended his hand. "We are to dance, first," he prompted. The faint smile that curved the handsome lips beneath the sandy moustache was not reflected in his eyes.

As if in a dream, True accepted his hand. And, with Michael holding her the proper arm's length from him, they gracefully circled the polished floor. Then as, remembering her part, True smiled shyly up at the tall, handsome man, she realized that all around them—but worlds away—a million other dancing couples whirled and swayed. The magic transformation was complete.

"You look ravishing—absolutely ravishing," Michael whispered. His voice, like the dancers, was worlds away. "That was a fitting introduction the mayor gave!"

The mayor? Oh, yes, the man Emily had stood beside had joined them—but what had he said? Something to do with her being rightfully named—"True North, the *true* owner of Magnolia Manor . . . shareholder . . . perhaps other holdings. . . ."

" 'Other holdings'?" Blankly, True repeated the words in search of an explanation.

Did Michael's arms tighten or had his body gone rigid? "Why, my claim on your heart."

True did not look up, and his voice, muffled by the whisper of feet against the marble floor, lost its tonal quality. "You have no claim on my heart, Michael."

Michael skillfully dodged a dipping couple. "You're saying I mean nothing to you?"

True missed a step, murmured an apology, then said slowly, "I didn't say that—but isn't this a strange place to be talking about—well, matters of the heart?"

"Yes!" And with the one word, he swung her inconspicuously past a group of nodding chaperones dozing against the wall, and onto the oleander-screened veranda.

Once alone, Michael allowed his arms to drop to his sides. "Have you reached a decision?"

"Have *you?*"

Michael groaned in the darkness. But True knew that the question had struck home. She had been right in thinking that he was weighing the pluses and minuses of a "nameless" wife.

"All right, *all right!* If we're going to be so brutally honest, I did want to make sure I could beat my wife with a clear conscience—not because of her lowly birth—" He paused, seeming to sense that his attempt to light-touch the words was out of keeping with the emotional strain between them. When True was silent, he said, "Well, you can understand that, can't you?"

"No—no, Michael, I can't. If you'd loved me, you would not have had to consider. But then," her voice dropped, for it was now that True realized something she, in her newfound glory, had failed to see clearly: "You never laid much claim on love, did you? You sought me out because of my holdings—I was a necessary piece to complete the railroad puzzle."

"My father wanted to find you!" His tone was defensive.

True, hardly hearing, went on more to herself than to him. "Then there was Magnolia Manor—and its undesirable people—'two birds with one stone'—finding me would solve everything—"

"That was Emily's concern, yes, but True—"

194

We should have talked like this long ago, some part of True was saying. The other was saying, "Never mind who was responsible for what. I am at fault, too. The 'Cinderella complex'—I almost succumbed, Michael."

"*Almost?* You mean you're turning us down? Any girl in her right mind would jump at this! Oh, True, listen to me—"

Turn *us* down, he had said. "Apparently your family is aware that you planned to marry me. Do they all know why? Will my decision disrupt their lives? Oh, I understand your father's tie with the past . . . but Emily's? How much stock does she hold?"

There was a silence. Then Michael said in a low voice. "She and I own the same number. Yours will be the swing vote."

"I see. Let's go back, Michael." Her voice, like her heart, was dead.

23

The Uninvited

It would be best if I tried to think of tonight as being like any other, so I can act natural, play out this role, and prepare for the stroke of 12. So thinking, True went through the motions of acknowledging introductions and managing to make small talk with the people around her. How would Emily and Michael dispose of them? Bring the story to a satisfactory conclusion? And the rest of the family? True realized with a jolt that she did not even remember their names. A family of which she was to have become a part—and she only recalled the names Oscar, Audrey Anne . . . and wasn't the rotund little man who quoted liberally from Edgar Allan Poe named Edgar, too?

Sometime during the evening, which seemed to run on and on, she caught sight of Inspector Keith's watchful eyes. And once Attorney Berkshire signaled as if he wished a word with her. But her mind was too muzzy to question presences, interpret signals, or make sense of anything. She felt feather-light. She was a piece of thistledown released from its pod. Drifting. Floating aimlessly. She was no longer the drab, insecure person Emily had taken her for. Neither was she the beautiful princess William St. John saw in his euphoric dream. She was True North, wanting with all her heart to get back to the balanced center of things—and not knowing how. And all the while, drifting. . . .

"Have you found Atlanta as you expected, Miss North?" "You will be staying, Miss North?" "How romantic, Miss North! Tell us how you ever came to meet our most eligible bachelor!"

Did she make sense as she moved from one group to another? The present was a dream. All the while, as she moved through it—her heart dead inside—her mind was trying to go back, to put events in order, so that the world would seem real.

Then, suddenly, the languor of unreality was shattered. There was the ear-splitting sound of a gun, followed by harsh voices outside. Somewhere a woman screamed. And the brilliant candles of the chandeliers paled in a cloud of smoke that billowed in from the open windows. Another shot . . . more hoarse voices of men outside . . . and then, in spite of the mayor's pleading for calm, there was a wild stampede in all directions.

Michael! Where was Michael! And Emily? With a pounding heart, True hurried about the room, which was emptying quickly. Unable to find either of them, she rushed up the stairs. Mr.

St. John's nurse may have left. He must not be alone.

Before making the turn to William St. John's suite, something compelled True to glance the opposite direction toward the guest room she occupied. There was indeed a twang of smoke in the halls, but she believed the source came from below. Michael's father would be in no immediate danger. But she or something she owned was! For in that one quick glance True saw that the door was open. Quickly, for fear her footsteps would be heard, she slipped off her shoes. Then she padded noiselessly in her stockinged feet, feeling her way in the darkness. At the door, she listened. No sound except for the hammering of her own heart.

When True was reasonably sure she was alone, she eased the door open a little wider and would have entered except that she stumbled over some seemingly large object. With a little cry, she fell helplessly to the floor, her leg twisted painfully beneath her. At first she was afraid the leg was broken, but when the pain subsided some, she pulled herself up by holding onto the chair over which she had stumbled, and felt her way to the table lamp. She hesitated and then lighted it, feeling sure that any intruder who meant to harm her would have made a move when she was at such a disadvantage.

The lamp flickered as if sharing her fear. Then, more certain of its safety, it bathed the room in light. What True saw caused her to raise a hand to her throat to choke back a scream of terror. The entire room was in disarray. Drawers of every desk, bureau, and dresser gaped open like fledglings waiting to be fed. The contents lay on the floor. Her precious letters, once neatly stacked, labeled, and tied with ribbon, were scattered about the room. Envelopes split, pages rumpled . . . and then her eyes came to rest on the French doors which opened onto a private balcony—wide open, the silk draperies fluttering inward. The avenue of escape the intruder used!

Taking no time to think, she hurried to the open doors. There, still dangling to the ground, was a knotted rope. This must mean that this person could be only moments ahead of her. Cupping her hands to her mouth, True called, "*Help!* HELP!"

The echo of her voice was only a ghostlike whisper against the hallway walls. And there it died away, unable to rise above the bedlam below, where many more people than appeared on the party's guest list were pushing, shoving, trampling one another in mass hysteria. What was it all about? Or did anybody know?

I ought to be helping, True thought. But, not understanding and in a state of shock and fear, she could only stand on the dark balcony in speechless horror.

When minutes—or was it hours?—later she would have turned, True finally found herself suddenly caught in a pair of strong arms, her own arms pinned to her sides. The face of her captor was indistinguishable. The thief? A murderer? An arsonist? It hardly mattered. No matter what the danger, she was unable to move.

"It's all right, True. It's all right."

Michael! She should feel relief. But she was incapable of any feeling whatsoever. With a shaking finger she pointed to the knotted rope.

"I know." Michael's voice sounded far off. "Just be thankful that your timing was a little off and you did not actually catch him in your room." He inhaled deeply and then continued, as if the words pained him. "And we can all be thankful that the rope's there—not shaped into a noose—"

Him, Michael had said. Who? And doing what in her room? But those questions were trivial in comparison . . . did her ears fail to hear or had Michael said the horrible word?

"*Noose?*" True could manage only the single word. She twisted to free herself, but Michael held onto her as if fearing she would make a wild attempt to climb down the rope herself and join the mob below. And maybe she would have, she realized later. For she was in such a state of lunacy that it was hard to bring meaning to Michael's obviously hurried explanation.

"Charles Devore . . . looking for something sent to you in the mail . . . tie him to the rob-

200

bery, but that fool kid . . . do you hear, True?" She heard but she did not understand.

The brooch? Mutely True nodded, trying hard to concentrate. ". . . irresponsible thing to do, withholding information *if* something reached you . . . and why, of all times, did you spread word of your alms? I thought those were to be done in secret!" His voice had grown bitter. "But, no, on the night of the ball . . . forgive me . . . not myself . . . maybe your foolishness saved a lot of lives. . . ."

The pain had returned to True's leg. The excitement, the pretense of it all, followed by the ugly fingers of fear that had squeezed her heart dry were too much. She swayed against Michael as her legs were about to give way beneath her. He enfolded her in his arms then, but True was unaware. So near was she to the netherworld of unconsciousness, she was able to discern only key words.

"Squatters came . . . crazy way of paying tribute . . . burning torches like savages . . . then threat of lynching. . . ." *Lynching?* ". . . warned you that the squatters don't 'belong' . . . till now. . . ." *Till now?* "Well" (reluctantly), "when Devore attempted to slip through the net set by officers, it was the squatters—*new owners by your decree*—they stopped them in their tracks! Suffice it to say that for a time there it appeared that the nooses and torches intended for them—well would be used on the self-appointed posse! A lynching in reverse . . . are you hearing?"

Now she heard—even understood. But she could not *believe!* What a peculiar chain of circumstances—no, *mysterious* was the word—brought this strange miracle about. The inspector-turned-traitor was in custody. Various agencies of the government would take over now, Michael explained, because the case involved a government payroll, money had been transported over state lines, and some other reasons True did not hear.

Her mind was on the brooch. Michael was sure to ask about it. What kind of answer could she give? Even though she expected it, when the question came True was still unprepared.

"Why did you deceive us, True? You could be helping to harbor a criminal, you know. The third robber, as far as we can ascertain, is still at large. Could you not have taken at least me into your confidence? Am I not to be trusted? Surely our relationship means *something!*"

True reeled uncertainly under the hammer-blows of his reasoning. With all her heart, she wished this man had no power over her—even when his reasoning fitted his own ends.

"Oh, Michael, try to understand—yes, of course, our relationship is important—but it has nothing to do with the brooch—and I still can't explain." *Brooch!* It was she who said it.

"Very well." Michael's voice was cold. He

dropped his arms to his sides as if granting permission for her to leave.

"I wish things were different—" True's words were cut short by blinding lights. Lighted lanterns, held high above the heads below, formed pools of light in the balcony, illuminating her face.

"Miss True North! Miss True North!" Voices chanted in unison. "Come down . . . come down. . . ."

With a thrill of joy in her heart, True turned a radiant face to the crowd of blacks, whites, sharecroppers, landlords . . . nobility and peasantry. The *grand monde* mingling with the uninvited. And it was the uninvited who, responding to some secret whisper of the Lord, found the courage to bring this miracle about.

The miracle enlarged. Even as True waved from the balcony and indicated with a downward-pointing of her finger that she would join the group, work-hardened hands linked with jeweled fingers to press into the great mansion. It was, True found herself smiling, as if the castle were under siege. By the Spirit of the Lord!

Again, lifting her blue-and-silver skirts, the Princess floated down the stairs—this time glancing over her shoulder only to make sure that Michael followed. At the landing, again she paused. Michael, as regal as any girl could expect a Prince Charming to be placed a hand lightly on her shoulder.

Then, ever the crowd-pleaser, he bowed. Smiling, as if whispering words of love, he said, "This, my dear, is your shining hour!"

Obediently, True smiled back. "The Lord's!" she corrected softly. Together they descended the remaining stairs.

So the Cinderella story was closing. Only, just as Young Wil changed the ending with each telling, the outcome had been unpredictable. Except that she wore no shoes! Then all such thoughts dissolved as True heard the beginnings of the most beautiful words she knew: "Amazing grace," timidly, then boldly, "how sweet the sound. . . ."

24

Missing Links

"Now that you've traced the missing links of your genealogy, I suppose you'll be leaving us?"

Nothing in Emily Kincaid's voice told True whether this woman wished her to stay, to go, or was indifferent to the decision. The two of them sat sharing tea in the conservatory, one of the few breaks either had taken since the party.

True set her empty cup on the carved ivory table in front of them. "Yes," she said simply, hoping the conversation would end.

Emily reached for a scone. "Tell me, have you accomplished what you hoped to? And learned what you intended?"

"More—much more. About myself. The world—"

"And love!" Michael's voice came from the door. Emily's cup clattered to the table in surprise. "You'll excuse me, ladies, but I do have three announcements to make. For one thing, the young lady here has turned down my proposal of honorable matrimony—" His voice was falsely light.

"Michael, please—" True tried to interrupt.

Michael was undaunted. "Second, the young

lady is to hear this! By special request, she is expected to remain here—my father's, yes—but add to it, the request of the United States Government. She will need to identify one Charles Devore *and*," he paused significantly, "declare any new evidence which may have reached her!" Dully, True realized that he should know the brooch was safe.

Emily's eyes sparkled with curiosity. When there was silence, she said, "You said three announcements, Michael."

"That I did," he answered, turning toward the door. "The third is to set all minds at rest. I shall not be gracing the premises for some time. There is much that needs attention concerning railroad business—particularly in light of our new findings. Rightful heirs. Divine rulers. And their kissing cousins."

The words, so stiffly spoken and formal, were intended to draw laughter or at least a smile, True supposed. Instead, they made her heart ache. Not for love of Michael, but for lack of it. And the fact that he was brokenhearted but stiffnecked in his pride. There was no way she knew to approach him. So thinking, his next words came as a great surprise.

"So will you pray for the state of my soul, Miss North?"

Oh, Michael, don't speak so lightly of so grave a matter. But aloud she said, "Of course, I will pray for all of you."

206

"Like you, I need to find some missing links—except that I'm not out searching!"

True turned away so that he would not see the tears in her eyes.

"It's my feeling that He's searching for you. Goodbye, Michael."

25

Solace on Thanksgiving

At first True was impatient with the delay. But she busied herself with the loose ends of her life here in Atlanta. Then, where once it had seemed to drag, time sped forward.

She spent as much time as possible with William St. John because she realized, even before the doctor told her, that there was little life within his frail body. His talk was fragmented, sometimes making little sense, and he often confused True with first her grandmother and then her mother. Her presence, however—by any name—never failed to fan the faint spark of his life. On one subject his mind was remarkably clear, his instructions concise: his will and his wishes concerning an unceremonial burial in the little churchyard adjacent to Magnolia Manor instead of the St. John plot.

"But your family?" True ventured once.

"*She* is my family. And now you are all I have left of her."

With tears in her voice, True explained over and over that, yes, the attorney had drawn up the papers properly for distribution of his property. It only upset the dying man when she begged that her name be stricken from his list of heirs, so in the end True saw that it was best to submit to his wishes, with two conditions.

He was to instruct Mr. Berkshire to notify the relatives prior to a reading of the will. To that he consented. Her second condition was that the money he wished her to have might be set aside legally in a special memorial fund. Her request came on one of Mr. St. John's bad days.

"Ah, yes," he agreed in a voice so faint True was hardly able to discern the words, "a stained-glass window in St. Mark's Cathedral—"

"No! I mean—please, *please* don't do that." True's voice was even fainter than his. He mustn't. Oh, he *mustn't!* Memory of the terrifying stained-glass art had been like plunging of a knife into her heart. "I want something living—something in which a part of you will go on. . . ." She groped for words, ". . . like the children you and my grandmother would have had—"

The wan face lighted in a way she had not seen before. "Bring him—*now!*" Accustomed to his fragmented speech, True was sure she understood. Calling Tisha, she asked the girl to summon the attorney. Shortly after the papers were drawn up and signed, designating the money to go into a medical research fund naming Wilson North, Jr., as guardian, William St. John slipped into a coma. Three days later he died with nobody knowing the exact whereabouts of his son.

Albert Berkshire, his usually merry blue eyes now sober, went over all the papers with True, explaining the parts she was unable to understand. Yes, he would be glad to handle her proxy in case anything came up here needing a vote regarding the railroad shares. True thanked him warmly, explained that she would be returning to Oregon as soon as the robbery investigation was over, and said a tentative good-bye. There were tears in his eyes. The good man was, she suspected, the only person besides her who mourned William St. John's passing.

To True's relief, Emily remained discreetly out of sight. "After all," true overheard her say in a voice pitched properly low, "there is a black wreath at the door." Which made the situation all the more depressing, seeing that none of the family had loved him.

Longing now to be out of the house and on her way home, True went shopping on two occasions. "Nothing perks up a lady's spirits like a new bonnet," Grandma Mollie always said. Well, a new outfit or so would be uplifting. She would be seeing the family . . . and, of course, Young Wil would meet her in Portland! Her clothing must be—well, convincing that she was indeed a grown-up young lady. Ready for love!

Her spirits soared as the saleslady helped her into what True blushingly admitted "very well may be my 'Going Away' dress. Wedding dress? No, she had one already. "My grandmother's —and it's never been worn!" True was to laugh as she shared that with Young Wil later. But at the time she was too giddy with happiness to wonder why the saleslady looked at her so strangely.

• • •

"We will not observe Thanksgiving since we're in mourning."

Emily Kincaid's flat announcement left True shaken. Not that the woman could any longer surprise her. Just the fact that Thanksgiving was here—and so was she. She should be home, where the air was filled with anticipation and the winey scent of cider-ready apples. Every woman in the settlement would be baking, and Grandma Mollie's brood would be scouring the walls of Turn-Around Inn in preparation for the holiday feast. Well, there was something she could do about the distance between. Wouldn't a telegram, delivered by a runner about the time O'Higgin said "*Amen*—now, dig in, folks!" be wonderful? But, she frowned, whoever heard of not *observing* Thanksgiving—even in the heart?

The day came and went. True was alone but not lonely. The telegram was on its way. She had written long letters to Aunt Chrissy and Young Wil and, for the first time in her life, written out

211

her prayer of thankfulness. Then, finding that she liked the words, she made a copy for Young Wil and tucked it into his letter.

One thing they *always* agreed on was the love of God—His tenderness, mercy, and love, which began, Young Wil explained, before He made the frame for the mountains or lighted the stars.

Dear Lord, I thank You for so much—most of all, Your patience while I shed bits and pieces of myself, trying to become some other person You never intended me to be. But thank You for Your *impatience,* too! I'm glad You woke me up before I cast off so much of what You molded that I no longer bore Your "likeness." My self-made punishment would have been the inability to go back to where I belong, Lord. Today, though I long for those I love, I am grateful in my chosen exile. Otherwise, Lord, I might have gone on with my "Cinderella fixation," placing hope on earthly things instead of *You* when life seemed bleak. Here I have found that I do not want glass slippers, Lord . . . just give me a pair of work boots and send me home. . . .

26

The Greatest Promise

True had dreaded the identification visit for so long that when it came she was almost disappointed in its anticlimactic brevity. Two clean-shaven, young officers—obviously in training —accompanied Investigator Keith. They were clumsy, and the older man made it his business to prompt them frequently.

Did this drawing resemble the man who conducted the first investigation concerning a Mr.—er—(one of the men consulted his notes) Devore? *Yes.* Did Miss North give him any information she had withheld from Mr. Keith? *No.* Then, because the matter had bothered her constantly, True said that it was quite the contrary. At their look of puzzlement, she opened her bag and drew out the brooch, which she had kept tucked away in a section of the original brown-paper wrapping.

"Meaning that I did not show him this." Her hand trembled as she held out the ornament. One of the three whistled softly in admiration. Otherwise, the men seemed surprisingly disinterested. "It came after we talked—"

Edward Keith shrugged. "No point in taking

213

it," he said, more to the other two men than to True. "The lady had described it already and it would have been returned to her."

The feelings of guilt were removed. True was first relieved and then puzzled. "But—but the sender—" she faltered, "you said—"

Running a hand through his thin, gray hair, the Chief Investigator seemed more preoccupied with a form he was completing than her words. At length he spoke. "They've all been apprehended, including a young man from Oregon. Ready, fellows?" He snapped his leather briefcase shut. "Case closed."

"Young man from Oregon," he had said. The words, so casually spoken, caused True to sway on her feet. As if seeing the awkward printing on the wrapping for the first time, she examined the letters. Of course! Why hadn't she noticed before that the *N* in North was upside down? And the eyes—those little-boy eyes that always looked to her and Young Wil for approval—could belong only to Marty! Little Marty, who had never been whatever it was he wanted to be but jumped on every bandwagon that passed through! Little Marty, who wanted to take justice in his own hands, who identified with Robin Hood's robbing the rich to help the poor! Running . . . running . . . out of breath, but running anyway. . . .

The men were moving toward the door.

"Wait!" True's voice sounded unreal to her own ears. "The boy—who was he?"

"Can't say for sure, but nothing for you to concern yourself with. First-timer, they say—opposing policies of the railroads. Probably get off lighter than he deserves."

When the men were gone, she sat down weakly—not knowing whether to laugh or cry. Why hadn't she recognized him? And how had she missed the little clues in letters from Aunt Chrissy and Young Wil? Maybe she hadn't wanted to see! Maybe—just *maybe*—Young Wil was right in saying she wasn't through growing up.

Well, she was growing! What she had learned here had given her a certain maturity of heart. And what she had done here would help so many, in both "homes."

A long sigh began at the tips of her toes and traveled the full length of her body, freeing her of the long-restrained guilt and fear. In its place was a gnawing hunger to be with her family to share their sorrow if Marty had been convicted; their joy, if the courts had seen fit to give him another chance. Everything was all right. Everything was so wonderfully all right!

True was filled with a joy that was like the spring rains that greened the Oregon meadows . . . the autumn sun that mellowed the fruit . . . warming her heart the way the sun warmed the earth after the winter cold.

"Thank You, Lord, thank You for all You've shown me. That I must stretch and grow . . . that life is for giving and the two words combined, *forgiving!* That the great tragedy in life is not death but what we allow to die within us while we live . . . let me take that thought with me . . . while leaving it here. . . ."

Two days later she was ready to leave. Her trunk was packed, her reservation made for the train ride back. And then came the surprise delivery. A special messenger brought her a package from Michael! The postmark was Boston.

It was, she realized, Michael's first gift to her. And his last. What had he chosen in farewell to a love that had never been? When the heavy outside wrappings fell away, True carefully removed the tissue from the small gold figurine and read the accompanying card.

"My gift to you—Statue of Aphrodite, Goddess of Love. Michael."

A little sadly, she rewrapped the statue and placed it carefully in the bag along with her gifts for Daddy Wil and Aunt Chrissy's twins. Then, removing one of the several copies of the New Testament she had purchased for the Sunday school class she undoubtedly would resume teaching, she wrote a note inside the cover.

"My gift to you—The Holy Bible, God of Love. True."

"The carriage is waiting!" Emily Kincaid's last command. Hosea picked up her bags.

True tried to thank Michael's cousin. "I'm grateful," she said, and tried to embrace her. There was no response, no bending toward love. Emily simply handed two letters to True and turned back to the dark corridors of the great house.

It was she—True realized—not herself, who must return to the "ashes." The ashes of a past she refused to leave. True sent up another silent prayer of thanksgiving to the Father who made it so clear that she could not—even to make a dying man happy—live out the life of her grandmother. Neither could she live out the life of her own mother here. And no fairy godmother was going to transform her into the girl Michael sought in the photograph.

She accepted Hosea's hand and stepped into the carriage. Only Jesus could save, heal, and make whole. He made no promise of "castle life" on earth.

Just love—the greatest promise of all!

27

Answer to a Prayer

Once the train journey began, True opened the letters she had clutched in her hand—not even trusting her handbag to care for them. The one from Aunt Chrissy she scanned hurriedly, knowing she would read it over and over before reaching Portland, where Young Wil would meet her. She had written him the date, then sent a telegram to make doubly sure he knew.

Her aunt's letter bubbled with happiness . . . True's arrival would be one of Miss Mollie's "rainbows formed by Oregon's mixture of sunshine and showers." True smiled mistily, understanding now, but what she did not understand was the liberal sprinkling of "the young Portland lady."

Young Wil had brought her to Turn-Around Inn for Thanksgiving . . . such a lovely girl . . . so alone, in need of understanding of the family. "You can be a great help to her—to both of them, True. Her name's Midgie—"

Midgie? *Midgie Callison!* True threw the letter onto the seat beside her, feeling her heart drop to the toes of her new pointed, button-down shoes, which were beginning to pinch.

There was no need to read further. True knew exactly how this "lovely girl" looked. She ought to—considering the distance between Portland and San Francisco! Midgie's conductor-father had used up the miles describing the "gray-green eyes slanting upward at the corners and heavy, dark hair done up fancylike." Why even *he* had given a hint that his daughter had a "young man." And his Midgie *had* to be "this young lady" in Young Wil's letters. And now Aunt Chrissy had referred to "both of them."

Well, we'll see about that, True thought furiously. *I can still bite, grown-up or not!*

Angrily, True ripped into the second letter. She had known it came from Young Wil and, foolish one that she was, had saved it (as always) in anticipation. Little had she known what the man she had loved all her life meant in his *heart* when he wrote of finding someone to take her place. Taking notes for him indeed! When it came to men, all women were just "ugly stepsisters" awaiting their chance to try on the glass slipper. . . .

Recognizing that she was in no mood to read, True began repeating the books of the Old Testament to gain control. "Genesis, Exodus, Leviticus. . . ." At "Joshua" she burst into laughter. Why, she was being pouty and jealous, *very* immature. And she was glad that Young Wil was not here to see such a mood.

She read the letter then, the laughter on her

lips dying and tears filling her eyes, transforming them blue to deep purple.

My darling: (*Darling! He'd said DAR-LING!*) I had a long talk with the Lord when your letter came, and this is in answer to your prayer. If, as you confessed, you've a "Cinderella fixation," it is I who put it there. I, your Prince. You see, not all Princes are rich and charming. But not all rich and charming Princes make tender, loving husbands. Riches cannot buy health, happiness, or heaven . . . but riches would make my dream of the research lab come true. For now, we must live on love with a cabin for a castle . . . happy forever after!

28

The True Magic of Love

The early-December sun dipped into the Western horizon. The days, having stretched their length, had shortened noticeably since True left. She had forgotten how quickly night fell in the mountains, blotting out everything but the glowing outlines of snow-capped peaks—and the glow within her heart.

Any moment now the train would come to a stop . . . and the moment had come! Love had led her home.

Quickly she smoothed imagined wrinkles from her dove-gray travel suit and touched the rosy softness of the feathered plume on her hat, hoping it was angled properly the way the milliner showed her. Almost unaware that her feet touched the ground, she made her way toward the station. *Wil . . . Wil . . . Wil!* The wild pumping of her heart was suffocating her. *Walk like a lady . . . stand tall . . . show him how you've grown up!*

But when she saw Young Wil's handsome face, lighted with those unforgettably expressive brown eyes focused on her and her alone, True let out a squeal of delight. And then, guided only by her heart, she was in his arms.

His strong arms closed around her possessively.

"Pardon me, I'm looking for an awkward girl in pigtails who has been known to bite!"

"And I," True's voice was muffled against his rough, wool-plaid jacket, "am looking for the most handsome, the most wonderful, the most *bossy* man in the state of Oregon!"

Young Wil laughed against the top of her head just beneath his chin.

"I'd say you've found your man!"

"Oh, yes, Wil—yes, *yes*, YES!"

"Here," he said, drawing a large handkerchief from his breast pocket. "You'll be crying any minute now."

"Wil North—" True began, then promptly burst into tears.

"Blow!" When she obeyed, Young Wil pulled her close to him again. "Such an advantage, knowing each other forever. This lifelong courtship's going to save a lot of red tape. Right?"

She snuggled closer. "If you say so," she said meekly.

And then fear gripped her heart. There was so much they had to talk about. Most of it could wait. But not this.

"Midgie?" Her whisper was faint.

"Ummm—you smell nice. Midgie? It's supposed to be a secret—but she and Marty are to be married Sunday, providing your train made it on time. Grandma Mollie's hinting that Turn-Around Inn's used to double weddings—so—?"

For the first time, his voice faltered. It was her turn to laugh.

"If you say so!"

There was no need for further words. Wrapped in each other's arms, they had found the true magic of love—one that grew slowly, steadily, recognizing no barriers.

Until two hearts beat as one. . . .